Options Trading Handbook

Mahesh Chandra Kaushik

SEBI Registered Research Analyst
SEBI Registration Number INH 100000908

"You may read thousands of books on options but you wouldn't find the knowledge that this book provides. All the writers are engaged in providing you descriptive knowledge of options, option Greeks etc. None of the books would provide you with the practical concepts on options that may enable even a semi-literate common waiter to use option trading to get rich. This book, which covers the latest information, right from the primary points or ABCs of options to option Greeks in a very simple language, is a rare work of Mahesh Kaushik, the most read research analyst of the Indian stock market".

DISCLAIMER

Investment/Trading in stock market is always risky and subject to market risks. I have attempted to provide in this book the best information as per my understanding, but before you decide to use any suggestion contained in this book, please do consider carefully. the risks involved and your risk bearing capacity.

I, Mahesh Chandra Kaushik, will not be responsible for any loss incurred as a result of any thing contained in this book.

If the name of any listed company, ETF or brokerage firm is used as an example in this book to make a point, it should be assumed that I am NOT making any recommendation in respect of that company or ETF or brokerage firm and I do not have any business interest in them, though there may be investments made by me or my wife in such a company, ETF etc.

All the characters and events referenced in the book are fictitious and have been used only to make the complex subject easily comprehensible. Still, any resemblance to a real name or person etc. should be treated as purely coincidental.

Options Trading Handbook

Mahesh Chandra Kaushik

Published by
PRABHAT PRAKASHAN PVT. LTD.
4/19 Asaf Ali Road,
New Delhi-110 002 (INDIA)
e-mail: prabhatbooks@gmail.com

ISBN 978-93-90378-54-8
OPTIONS TRADING HANDBOOK
by Shri Mahesh Chandra Kaushik

Edition
2025

Price
₹ 300.00 (Rupees Three Hundred only)

Printed at
Narula Printers, Delhi

Preface

My dear readers,

Greetings to you all.

My fifth book on the stock market is in your hands. My first three books were written from the point of view of investment in stock markets keeping small investors in mind, and your great admiration for the fourth book "41 Tips for Success in Stock Market" made the same, the best seller book on stock market.

The readers among you who have gone through any of the four books on investments written by me know that I like to explain complex subjects in simple language. Keeping the same thing in mind, this book also has been written like a novel in the format of a story to ensure you don't get bored at any point while reading it.

In fact, I am not a great writer or investor. I am also a common man just like you. I started investing in stock market in the year 2005 and I just offer my tips based on my experiences with the market. Your liking for my blog and your faith in the same kept on getting stronger and you only made me a writer.

I feel overwhelmed by the kind of support from all of you for my YouTube channel and the kind of appreciation you have showered on my previous books. It was the overwhelming demand from you readers that forced my pen to write this book on option trading.

I hope a thorough reading of this book with full attention and concentration would help you earn money through option trading in the stock market. Still, you should keep in mind that **trading in stock market is not a science; instead it is an art and learning an art demands practice.** Hence, for reading this book also, you need to apply the same level of devotion and hard work that you use for reading course books to succeed in your examinations.

I hope, with the help of this book, you would grow to be a successful option trader, even more successful than Ghisu Bhai, and would definitely share your success stories with me on my email id mahesh2073@yahoo-com.

Now, it's time to offer my thanks. **First of all, for successful completion of this work, I am grateful to the Supreme Being that you may know by any of the names like God, Allah, Wahe Guru or Bhagwan, but that is the creator of the entire world and that only is the Supreme Power and He only has chosen me to guide small investors on stock markets. With that thought in my mind, I dedicate this book also, like all my previous books, to that Supreme Power, the Lord of this infinite Universe.**

Next, I am indebted to my Gurudev Parampujya Shri Shri 1008 Satyanarayanji Falahari Maharaj, Sartaneshwar Mandir, Lotana who has provided direction to the boat of my life with his spiritual patronage on many occasions.

Thirdly, I am thankful to my wife Smt. Seema Kaushik who also runs a cooking channel on YouTube in the name of Seema Ki Rasoi. She never stopped me from taking risks in stock markets. Before discovering the successful technique for option trading, I used her account many times for testing various methods in practice and before arriving at the final technique, I even squandered her money on several occasions.

But she always kept me motivated. She insisted that it was only a learning process and kept me assured that I was one day going to find out the right method for option trading that would do good to lacs of people and hence that money was being used for the benefit of those people only. **It was not possible for me to write this book without her energy and generosity.**

Fourthly, I am heartily obliged to Shri Piyushji of Prabhat Prakashan who provided me a platform to publish printed editions of my books and played the role of a great facilitator for making my books easily available to my followers by getting them translated in English and other languages. Shri Piyushji kept on chasing me like a brother with his loving reminders for completion of the book; that kept me always under pressure to take necessary time out of my busy schedule for writing this book.

And lastly, **thanks to all you readers and a lac of followers of my YouTube channel who always expressed their affection and confidence in me with their comments that helped me rise from a common investor to the best-selling author on stock markets.**

May God bless us all!!

Respectfully yours,

Mahesh Chandra Kaushik
Assistant Revenue Accounts Officer
Office of District Collector, Sirohi, Rajasthan

Registered Office
Mahesh Chandra Kaushik,
Research Analyst
J J Colony Pindwara, 307022,
District Sirohi, Rajasthan

Contents

1

Ghisu Bhai—An Introduction

Ghisu Bhai worked as a waiter in Chamunda Mata Ice Cream Parlour. This was a famous ice cream parlour and his job covered tasks like taking orders from customers, serving ice cream on their tables and returning empty cups, papers and plates left behind by the customers to dustbins and washbasins.

Unfortunately, Mahesh Kaushik, Research Analyst (I, the author of this book), lived very close to that ice cream parlour.

This is being termed as unfortunate, as investment in stock market is an infectious disease like Corona or COVID-19. When you find any of your friends or colleagues earning money by investing in the stock market, you may also get infected by that stock-market-borne disease.

This disease is quite dangerous. Even if any of your friends, neighbours or any of your enemies, instead of making money, incurs heavy losses in the stock market, you get into the grip of this disease insisting that the other guy was unlucky, was a fool and did not know how to trade with prudence, and you are not like him, rather you are quite clever and hence you would surely make money.

Thus, whenever Chandu and Chinki (In my previous book "**How Chandu Earned and Chinki Lost in the Stock Market**", Chandu is my fictitious follower in the stock market and he invests as per my guidance and Chinki is his wife) came to visit me at my residence, they would also go to Chamunda Ice Cream Parlour to enjoy ice creams. There, Ghisu Bhai would overhear their talks and try to pick up tips for the stocks that might help him earn unexpected returns.

As half-baked knowledge is dangerous, investments made on the basis of these tips heard on the grapevine kept on resulting sometimes in loss and sometimes in profit for Ghisu Bhai. The net result was nil.

However, when Ghisu Bhai found that Chandu's driver Md. Andul Ajeej Saheb also turned a multimillionaire with the help of regular investments in stocks, he just got puzzled. One day, when Abdul Ajeejji, along with his wife and son Md. Kareem, came to the parlour to have ice creams, Ghisu Bhai felt delighted and decided to take the tip from him for the stock that would make him also a multimillionaire. That's it! Ghisu Bhai, without wasting any time, cleaned his table thoroughly and served his order promptly. When Abdul Ajeej Bhai offered him tip while leaving, Ghisu Bhai said with folded hands, "Uncle, I don't want tip from you. You have become so successful in a very short time. Hence, instead of money as a tip, please give me tips for the stocks that you are buying these days". Abdul was in a hurry. While getting into his car, he just said, "I trade only in options these days".

Perfect! Ghisu Bhai memorised the name—option... option...option. He called his broker the next day, "Could you please check how much balance is available in my account?"

"Around 26,150".

"Leaving a balance of Rs. 1000, please buy shares of 'Option' company for the rest of the amount". Ghisu Bhai instructed his broker.

The broker was utterly confused to hear the instruction. The broker told Ghisu Bhai that there was no company in the name of 'Option' and option was a kind of contract where two individuals enter into a deal to buy or sell a stock at a specific price.

Now, it was Ghisu Bhai's turn to get confused. He just wondered what the hell this option was. He quickly cudgelled his brain and recollected the name of an adviser who was always ready to help him for free.

He asked his parlour manager for an hour's break, got five nice *kesar-pista* ice cream cones packed, rushed to my house and pressed the doorbell. I was a bit surprised to see Ghisu Bhai, wondering what had made him come to my house without any invitation. Had he come to borrow some money? I was scared of that the most!

Ghisu Bhai said, "Saab, Namaste! It's Sunday today; hence I have brought ice cream cones for you".

"But, dear, I never ordered for any ice cream!"

"You have not ordered, Saab. This I have brought as a gift".

"But I don't take ice cream at all".

"It's ok, Saab. Bhabhiji and children would have it. You are five members in the family; hence, I have brought 5 cones. You also please have it today on my behalf".

"But what's the occasion today? Why are you so kind today?"

"Nothing Saab. You are so nice; you guide everybody for free. After all, we also have some duty towards you".

I was now able to make out everything. Ghisu Bhai had to earn money from the stock market and he was here to ask for some tips. And now he would not allow me to relax even on holidays and would keep bothering me daily. Hence, I said, "Look, Ghisu Bhai. I will not give you any tip. If you want to buy stocks, please go and read my blogs and keep watching my YouTube channel and then invest in small amounts using the methods suggested by me".

"Sir, I assure you I am not here to ask for any tip. You just kindly let me know the BSE and NSE codes for 'Option' company, as I have to buy shares of that company and my broker is telling that there is no company with that name".

I could by now understand that somebody had suggested Ghisu Bhai to trade in options and he had assumed that to be a stock. After knowing the entire thing, I thanked Ghisu Bhai for the ice cream cones and asked my son to keep the same in our fridge.

I respectfully offered Ghisu Bhai a seat and explained to him, "Your broker is right. Actually, there is no company with the name as 'Option' and option is only a segment in the stock market. Just as stocks are traded, the derivatives of stocks are also traded. These are referred to as futures and options or derivative trading by the traders".

"Sir, I want to learn this option trading".

"Ghisu Bhai, I feel quite scared of learners like you, as I don't appreciate the principles that you people follow in the stock market. For example, you invest in falling stocks and then remain locked with them for even up to six years. You also try to average that falling stock just to prove your ego right. All these things demonstrate that you do not possess the qualities of a good trader. If I go on to teach you futures and options, not only you would be doomed to failure but I would also become a laughing stock".

I could see Ghisu Bhai's eyes getting watery. He said, "Sir, I had heard that you are the man to selflessly help small investors in the stock market. I also sometimes watch your videos on YouTube channel; they arouse feelings of affinity and kinship.

You have made Chandu and Abdul Ajeej successful investors in the stock market. It's ok if you still want to send me back disappointed...!"

I also got overwhelmed with sadness after looking at the tearful eyes of Ghisu Bhai. I immediately apologised to him for being so blunt and said, "Hey Ghisu Bhai, you are like my kin only. I have unselfish love for you also as much as I have for my family members or my followers. Not only that, I even love those new traders who vilify me through their comments on my YouTube channel and my blog".

Yes, it's true. I do not feel annoyed with those among the people offering their comments on my blog and YouTube channel who sometimes express their views in disparaging languages; rather I love them also. I feel they write such expletives possibly because they still lack the maturity that I expect in trading and investments.

My words provided some comfort to Ghisu Bhai. He said, "Then please teach me option trading".

"But I have some conditions that you would have to agree".

"I am ready for any condition".

"The first condition is that you would not call me every now and then and try to learn over phone. I will spare 1 hour for you on Sundays only".

"I agree to that".

"The second condition is that, immediately after learning, you would not straightaway jump into option market; you would practice with paper trading for a month to start with".

"What is this paper trade?"

"Paper trade refers to fictitious trades done on paper only".

"OK, I accept this condition also".

"While teaching you, I would also ask you to do some homework like school children. Every Sunday, when you come here, you would bring your last homework duly completed; I would take up further lessons only after ensuring that".

"OK, I agree to this condition also".

"Great! In that case, you are welcome at 10 am next Sunday. I will teach you how to earn with options".

With that, I saw Ghisu Bhai off that day.

What did we learn from this chapter?

Derivatives market refers to the segment of the stock market where derivative contracts based on stocks are traded. In other words, instead of buying and selling stocks or indexes directly, the contracts based on them are bought or sold in this market.

The derivatives segment of the market is called Futures and Options or F&O.

It's necessary to do homework to learn option trading, and at least a month's practice in fictitious trades based on the strategy propounded in this book is essential to be able to earn profits in options.

□

2

Basic Information on Option Trading

Ghisu Bhai came next Sunday and I started to teach him ABCs of option trading.

"Ghisu Bhai, what would be the total value of ice creams stored in your Chamunda Ice Cream Parlour at this time?"

"Sir, our Sethji normally stores all the variations in almost all branded ice creams. We have several deep fridges and tables. Hence, our parlour has any time ice creams worth at least Rs. 10 lacs".

"So, your Sethji would have bought these ice creams by paying cash?"

"No, he picks up these ice creams on credit and pays only 10% to the trader as advance. Final payments are made only after one or two months".

"That means, only Rs. 1 lac of Sethji's capital is blocked against the stock of Rs. 10 lacs. In other words, if Sethji earns a profit of 20% on these ice creams, he would have made Rs. 2 lacs i.e. 20% of Rs. 10 lacs. Right?"

"Yes, that's correct".

"That means, he earned a profit of Rs. 2 lacs on his investment of Rs. 1 lac. This comes to 200% profit".

By now, Ghisu Bhai was terribly bored. He said, "Sir, you are going back on your word. I have come here to learn option trading, but you are, by showing me 200% profit in the business of ice creams, trying to suggest me to open my own ice cream parlour".

I laughed, "No dear, I am just trying to make you understand the **Power of Leverage**—the first part of option trading".

I continued, "Power of leverage refers to 'power of credit'. In other words, the power of leverage is the power to enable a small amount of capital to create a business ten times its value. Suppose the shares of a company X are trading at Rs. 410. How much capital would you need to buy 2000 shares of that company X?"

"410 multiplied by 2000 i.e. Rs. 8,20,000".

"Perfectly right. Now if you sell these stocks when the price goes up by Rs. 40, you would make a profit of Rs. 80,000 that is approximately 10% of your invested capital.

"However, in the case of option trading, you would need only Rs. 40,000 to enter into a deal for a position of 2000 shares in the same company by paying a premium of approximately Rs. 20 per share (premium is fluctuating; things would be getting more and more clear as you go on reading this book).

"If the price of the share goes up by Rs. 40, you would get Rs. 80,000 for 2000 shares @ Rs. 40 per share on the settlement day (don't panic, as you progress, it would be clear what a settlement day means).

Update: *This part of the book was written in 2017 when option deals were settled in cash. SEBI has since changed the rules and now in 2020, cash settlement is available only for deals involving indexes like NIFTY or Bank NIFTY. Deals for the rest of stocks are now settled by physical delivery. That means, you would have to either sell your option contract few hours before its expiry or take physical delivery of underlying stocks* *in your demat account if you have bought call and the call is In the Money.*

"Though your real profit would be Rs. 40,000 only as you had paid a premium of Rs. 40,000 to buy this position, this profit would be 100% of your invested capital. This is just to explain that you may, by exploiting the power of leverage, earn profit almost 10 times more that earned in cash market".

"But, what if the stock price goes down?"

"In that case your entire premium i.e. Rs. 40,000 would be lost".

"My God, this is quite dangerous! I am not interested in learning option trading. You may not know but I never book loss. I am in the market for the last 10 years and have never incurred any loss of even one rupee. My stocks do fall sometimes, but even in that case, I hold the same for 3 to 5 years. Sometime or other during that period, I manage to exit only after making a profit of 100 to 150 rupees".

I explained to Ghisu Bhai, "That is the reason that you have not been able to make any profit in the stock market during the last 10 years.

"Investment in options, if handled with prudence, is safer compared to investment in stocks.

"If investment is made in options in a proper way (Complete details of the method will be explained later in this book. Hence, it's my advice that you don't raise doubts today without going through the entire book.), this investment is much safer than buying stocks in cash market and holding the same. Also, investment in option is even safer than buying futures contracts".

"But sir, you only just said that I may lose the entire premium of Rs. 40,000. How is it safe then?"

"Ghisu Bhai, let me impart to you the basic information on

option before I explain that. You would be able to understand all this later. Just relax.

"Before I go ahead to explain option, we would need to link this to something in our real world. That would help you to understand this.

"Imagine there is a large trader in the market who deals in potato and buys as well as sells potato.

"Now, you think that the market rate of potato, that is currently selling at Rs. 20 per kg, is going to go up, and if you buy potato now and sell the same after 1 or 2 or 3 months, you may earn profit.

"So, you go to that trader (his name is Shivlal Thekedar) to buy potato in cash. He buys or sells a minimum of 400 bags at a time. 400 bags with 100 kg in each bag i.e. 40000 kg of potato is the minimum quantity that you would have to buy. Thus, you would need Rs. 8 lacs in cash to buy 40000 kg of potato @ Rs. 20 per kg.

"Here, '400 bags' is the 'lot size'. Yes...if you read lot size anywhere in reference to option trading, this is what it means. For example, NIFTY has lot size of 75 in options, i.e. you would have to buy or sell at least 75 NIFTY together. Lot size for IOC stocks is 1500. Lot size for Infosys is 500.

"In fact, these lot sizes are decided by stock exchanges and these sizes even get revised depending on the rise and fall of the underlying stock prices. Exchanges try to keep the value of lot size between Rs. 5 lacs and Rs. 10 lacs. Thus, if the lot size of a stock is 2000 and its market price is Rs. 380, the total price of the lot comes to Rs. 7,60,000. Similarly, if market rate of NIFTY is Rs. 10000 and its lot size is 75, the market price of its lot would be Rs. 7,50,000.

"The main aim of the exchanges to keep the price of a lot over Rs. 5 lacs is to keep small investors away from futures and options, as generally, small investors do not show prudence while trading in futures and options and, instead of treating it as a business, use it like gambling and lose all their money".

Ghisu Bhai said, "Sir, my heart is sinking. Neither I do have 5 to 8 lacs of rupees nor do I want to lose all my money. Hence, thank you for all the knowledge that you have imparted. I now feel that I may earn more money just by working some overtime at the ice cream parlour itself".

"Oh dear, you don't need a seed capital of 5 to 8 lacs of rupees for option trading. I can teach you to trade in options even with an amount of Rs. 50,000 only, and don't get worried, you would not lose all your money when you trade following my techniques".

"Then it's ok," said Ghisu Bhai, feeling satisfied.

"Now imagine that Shivlal Thekedar provides you facility of option trading in potato. In other words, if the current market rate of potato is Rs. 20 per kg, he sells you calls for different values, say 20, 22, 24, 26, 28, 30 etc. by charging some premium per kg. Suppose you buy his 'call' of Rs. 22 per kg. It actually means that he charges premium, say @ 30 paise per kg, totalling Rs. 12,000 for 40,000 kg of potato and enters into a contract with you to sell you 40,000 kg of potato @ Rs. 22 per kg on the last Thursday of the month.

"Here, the last Thursday of the month is the expiry date. In Indian stock markets also, the last Thursday of every month only is treated as expiry date for options under option trading. Some options like NIFTY and Bank NIFTY have even weekly expiries, i.e. they expire every Thursday.

"Suppose the market rate of potato goes up to Rs. 24 per kg on the last Thursday of the month. And, you have already bought a call for Rs. 22 from Shivlal Thekedar. That means you have a deal to buy potato @ Rs. 22 per kg. Thus, you buy 40,000 kg of potato @ Rs. 22 per kg and sell the same in market for Rs. 24 per kg, thus earning a sum of Rs. 80,000 @ Rs. 2 per kg.

"You had invested an amount of Rs. 12,000 and you have made a profit of Rs. 80,000 as above, hence your net profit after adjusting the premium of Rs. 12,000 comes to Rs. 68,000 only".

"What if the market rate of potato were Rs. 25 per kg on the expiry date?" asked Ghisu Bhai.

"In that case, you would have received Rs. 1,20,000 @ Rs. 3 per kg from your option trade, and after adjusting your premium of Rs. 12,000, you would have made a net profit of Rs. 1,08,000".

"But sir, I would not have made even a single rupee because, if I had entered into a deal to buy 40,000 kg of potato @ Rs. 22 per kg, I would have had to first buy that 40,000 kg of potato from Shivlal Thekedar on expiry date and I would have required Rs. 8,80,000 for the same.

"Neither will there be 9 maund of oil nor will Radha dance. Neither do I have Rs. 8,80,000 with me nor could I have bought potato on expiry nor I could have sold the same @ Rs. 25 per kg to make Rs. 10 lacs".

I comforted him, "Hey Ghisu Bhai, don't get worried. A lot of misinformation relating to option trading is flying about. In fact, there are two types of call options:

First, European style call option where physical delivery is not required, deals are settled in cash and you are free to exercise the option before expiry.

Second, American style call option where physical delivery of stocks does take place and you also don't have option to exercise the option before expiry.

"India has adopted the European style of option trading, meaning that you may buy and sell option contracts before expiry just like stocks. Also, all deals in Index options like NIFTY and Bank NIFTY are settled in cash on expiry date and physical delivery is not involved. In the case of a deal involving any other stock, the same is settled through physical delivery. If you want to get the same settled in cash, you would have to either sell your option contract few hours before expiry or, if you have bought call and the same is In the Money, you would have to take physical delivery of that stock in your demat account".

"Sir, I didn't follow anything! What is that expiry and what is settlement? Whatever you are telling is going over my head".

"OK Ghisu Bhai. I will have to explain to you in potato language only. Suppose the market rate of potato is Rs. 20 per kg. You feel that this rate would go up, meaning that, in the language of the stock market, you are bullish on potato. So, you buy a call option of March series with strike price of '20' from Shivlal Thekedar".

"Sir, what's this March series?" interrupted Ghisu Bhai.

"Hey, deals may be made 3 months in advance in futures and options. For example, it's the month of March running now and if you enter into a contract for the last Thursday of March, it would be referred to as March series.

"But, if you so wish, you may trade for the last Thursday of April or May and the same would be called April series or May series".

"That's right, sir".

"Now, you have bought the call of March series of potato with strike price of Rs. 20 per kg. Shivlal Thekedar charges you a premium of Rs. 2.20 per kg and you have to buy a minimum of 40,000 kg as a lot. Thus, you have to pay 40,000 × 2.20 = 88,000 rupees as premium to him. The last Thursday of March is the date of settlement of this deal; this would be referred to as the expiry date.

"Suppose the rate of potato goes up to Rs. 23 per kg immediately after your trade for the above call. As the rate goes up, the premium on call option also goes up. Suppose the premium on the call goes up from Rs. 2.20 to Rs. 3.20. In that case, without waiting for the expiry date (under European style call option of the Indian stock market), you may sell this contract just like stocks to another buyer with premium @ 3.20 per kg and get 40,000 × 3.20 = 1,28,000 rupees, thus making a net profit of Rs. 40,000 after adjusting Rs. 88,000 towards the premium paid. Had you waited for settlement on expiry on the last Thursday of March and if the closing market rate on that day were Rs. 30 per kg, exchange would have paid you Rs. 4,00,000 towards 40,000 kg @ Rs. 10 per kg (30 – 20) through settlement in cash (only for European call option CE prevalent in India currently). You may make out that your net profit would have been only Rs. 3,12,000 after adjusting Rs. 88,000 paid as premium. Even brokerage and STT (Securities Transaction Tax) would have to be adjusted to compute actual profit".

"But, what if the rate of potato falls to Rs. 21.30 on expiry?"

"In that case, you would receive settlement at the rate of 21.30 – 20 = 1.30 per kg, that is 40,000 × 1.30 = 52,000 rupees. But you have already paid Rs. 88,000 to Shivlal Thekedar towards premium; hence you would incur a loss of 88,000 – 52,000 = 36,000 rupees and brokerage and STT".

"And if the rate remains Rs. 20 per kg?"

"In that case, you would not get anything and your entire premium of Rs. 88,000 would be lost".

"What if the market rate of potato falls to 19, 18, 17 or 10 or even to 5, 4, 3 or 2 rupees per kg or only one rupee per kg, what would be my loss?" asked Ghisu Bhai.

"Even in that case, your loss would be limited to the maximum of the premium of Rs. 88,000 paid by you; this is the beauty of a call option. It gives you a right to buy at a fixed price but you are not bound to exercise that right. If potato is selling at any rate below Rs. 20 per kg, you would not exercise your right to buy potato @ Rs. 20 per kg from Shivlal Thekedar and he, who is the call writer, will get the entire premium amount of Rs. 88,000. Thus your loss in that call option remains limited to the premium paid by you.

"By buying a call option, you get a right to buy stocks at a fixed strike price irrespective of the prevailing rate on the date of settlement. Thus, if the rate is above your strike price, you exercise your right; you may realise unlimited profits by doing that.

"But, in a call option, you are not obligated to exercise your right. In other words, if the market rate is below your strike price on the date of settlement, you would not exercise your right and you incur the maximum loss of the premium paid by you.

"This is a kind of insurance where you pay a premium and, in return, receive a right to buy underlying stock at a fixed strike price without any obligation. You are free to use or not to use that right. The person selling the call option (call writer) gets the premium paid by you. His profit is limited; the maximum he gets is the premium paid by you. But if the price goes up, he would have to pay you the difference amount irrespective of the level of price; hence the loss to the call writer is unlimited".

"Sir, your words do not give me any indication that this is a safe method. I am sweating to even hear that the premium amount of Rs. 88,000 referred to in your example. Firstly, I don't have that much to pay that premium amount and secondly, I don't have the courage to lose that entire amount of Rs. 88,000," said Ghisu Bhai.

"Look, Ghisu Bhai. This is just an imaginary case. You don't need Rs. 88,000 to buy call and put options in the market. The lot size for NIFTY is 75 and if you buy a call at a premium of Rs. 100, you would just need Rs. 7500 for the same. Similarly, the premium is also different for different strike prices. Let's take an example of an Out of the Money (OTM) call. Suppose NIFTY is currently at 10,150 and out of its strike prices like 10,200, 10,250, 10,300, 10,350, 10,400, 10,450 and 10,500, you buy a call in the upper range i.e. an OTM call, you may possibly get the same even at a premium of just Rs. 5 or Rs. 10 i.e. for a total of 75 × 10 = 750 rupees only. Buying an OTM call of this nature is like buying a lottery ticket. If market goes through a big bounce and NIFTY reaches somewhere near 10,500 even before expiry, the premium of your call of 10,500 also would go up from Rs. 10 to Rs. 100-150 straightaway. But, possibility of that happening is quite rare and most of the novice investors keep on buying such cheap OTM calls like lottery tickets and losing their premiums.

"But in fact, if this Out of the Money call/put trades are made following the call-put ratio strategy, it may earn profits. Details of the same are discussed in subsequent chapters of this book".

"Sir, what is an Out of the Money (OTM) call?"

"Calls are of three types:

(a) In the Money (ITM)
(b) At the Money (ATM), and
(c) Out of the Money (OTM).

"For example, if NIFTY is currently at 10,150, a call option with strike price of 10,100 already has a profit of Rs. 50 and hence it's called In the Money (ITM) call. A call of Rs. 10,150 has its strike price equal to the current market price and hence does not involve any immediate profit or loss; this is called 'At the Money' (ATM) call. And, in the case of a call of Rs. 10,200, the market price is on the contrary less than the strike price; hence such a call is called 'Out of the Money' (OTM) call.

"Taking the example of potato, if the current market price of potato is Rs. 20 per kg and you buy a call of Rs. 24 per kg from Shivlal Thekedar, that would be Out of the Money (OTM) call. Shivlal would charge lower premium for the same, as profit in this call is possible only when the market price of potato goes above Rs. 24 per kg. As the chances of that happening are lower, Shivlal is ready to offer the call at lower premium.

"In fact, the rate of a call or a put keeps on fluctuating in the option market till the date of expiry. Thus, if you have bought an ITM (In the Money) call or put and you sell the same before expiry, you don't lose your entire premium. For example, suppose NIFTY is currently at 10,165 and the gaps between strike prices of NIFTY are 50-50. Thus, a call of 10,150 is an ITM (In the Money) call and that of 10,200 is an OTM (Out of the Money) call.

"You expect NIFTY to go up by the date of expiry and you buy a NIFTY call of 10,150 by paying a premium of Rs. 123, thus making a total payment of 123 × 75 = 9225 rupees. Now, if NIFTY falls and trades at 10,088 2-3 days before expiry on the last Thursday of the month, your call of 10,150 effectively turns into an OTM (Out of the Money) call and its premium also may go down to Rs. 78.

(Please note that this is just an imaginary case and premium of 78 can't be computed based on any formula, as just like the prices of stocks, premiums for calls also depend on the demand and supply of buyers and sellers.)

"If you believe that NIFTY would not go above 10,150 till the expiry, you may sell your call at the rate of 78, thus getting a total of 75 × 78 = 5850 rupees. Your loss is then limited to 9225 – 5850 = 3375 rupees only.

"If you decide not to sell your call, your loss is still limited to the amount of premium i.e. Rs. 9225 paid by you, irrespective of the extent of fall in NIFTY on the date of expiry.

"However, suppose NIFTY rises to 10,300. It's then natural that the premium on your call of 10,150 also goes up to say somewhere near Rs. 233. You may then exit without waiting for the expiry by selling your call at 233, thus taking a total amount of 233 × 75 = 17,475 rupees. In this case, you earn a profit of around 17,475 – 9225 = 8250 rupees. You may have to adjust brokerage to arrive at the net profit.

"Lastly, if you buy a NIFTY call of 10,150 by paying a premium of 123 and hold the same till expiry, and NIFTY closes at 9850 on the last Thursday of the month, you would not get anything and you would, at most, lose the premium paid by you.

"Hope it's now clear to you that the call bought by you was actually a right to buy NIFTY at 10,158 on expiry. But, as the market rate of NIFTY went down to 9850, you did not exercise your right and hence the premium paid by you to acquire that right went to the call writer. Your loss was limited to the premium paid.

"But, had NIFTY closed at 10,453 on expiry, the exchange, as part of its settlement process where it makes payment of the difference amount to all ITM (In the Money) call and put holders, would have paid you at the rate of 10,453 – 10,150 = 303 for the lot size of 75, the total being 75 × 303 = 22,725 rupees less around Rs. 1000 towards STT (Securities Transaction Tax), stamp duty and brokerage.

"Had NIFTY closed on 10,150 only with a marginal profit for you, Broker would have given option to you to exercise your call. Here, option to exercise means exercising your right to buy under the call. As the profit available to you would have been only 8 × 75 = 600 rupees, against around Rs. 1000 payable towards STT etc., you would have incurred a loss of around Rs. 400 if you had gone ahead to exercise your right.

"I hope you now understand call option properly. The other kind of option is called put option.

"What is PUT option?

Put option entitles you the right to sell at a specified strike price. Let's get back to our example of potato. The current market rate for potato is Rs. 20 per kg. You feel there is going to be a bumper crop of potato this year that may bring down its price in the market. You hence buy a put option in potato with a strike price of Rs. 20. The market rate of potato falls to Rs. 16 per kg on the date of expiry. You as a holder of above put option, have the right to sell potato @ Rs. 20 per kg. You thus earn a profit of 20-16 = 4 rupees per kg.

"Just like calls, puts also come with different strike prices, and premium on a put also keeps fluctuating. Puts also are of three kinds.

1. Out of the Money Put
2. At the Money Put, and
3. In the Money Put.

"Let's now take the example of NIFTY straightaway. NIFT is currently at the level of 10,200. If you buy a put option of 10,200 in April options series by paying a premium of 165, this would be 'At the Money' put, as the strike price for the same is neither in profit nor in loss presently. You would have to pay 75 × 165 = 12,375 rupees as premium for the same.

"Suppose NIFTY closes on the date of expiry down at 10,035. In that case, exchange would pay you, as the owner of above put option, at the rate of 10,200 – 10,035 = 165, a total amount of 165 × 75 = 12,375 rupees that is just equivalent to your premium amount. In other words, if NIFTY goes down up to 10,035, you would neither earn any profit nor incur any loss (in fact, you may incur some loss towards payment of brokerage and taxes).

"If NIFTY closes still lower, say 10,000, on the date of expiry, you would receive 75 × 200 = 15,000 rupees, thus resulting in a profit of around Rs. 2500 after adjusting premium, brokerage and taxes.

"If NIFTY goes up from 10,200 to 10,300, 10,500, 10,700, 11,000, 12,000 or any level above, as a put holder, your loss is limited to the premium paid by you. On the contrary, your profit is unlimited. If you buy put with a strike price of 10,200 and NIFTY goes down to 9,200, you would get (10,200 – 9,200 = 1000) × 75 = 75,000 rupees.

"Similarly, if NIFTY is at 10,200 and you buy a put of 10,300, NIFTY is already down by 100 points from your strike point of 10,300. In other words, your put is already in profit of 100 points. This kind of put is called 'In the Money' put. You may have to pay a higher premium for such a put. If you can acquire 'At the Money' put of 10,200 by paying a premium of 165, the premium for the put of 10,300, considering the profit already existing, may be around 265.

"I want to emphasise again that premium is not a fixed value. Premium fluctuates just like prices of stocks and this also works on the principle of demand and supply. Thus, if the market trends upwards i.e. market moves in bull phase, the premium on calls go up, and when the market trends downwards i.e. market enters bear phase, the premium on puts go up. Also, the premium is high at the start of a series, as the time available up to expiry is more for the same and you have better chances of making profit. The more the expiry is closer, the less is the premium. I will explain this in detail in a subsequent chapter.

"If NIFTY is at 10,200 and you buy a put option of 10,100, you are not going to get anything even if NIFTY goes down to a level of 10,100. This put is called 'Out of the Money' put. Naturally, the premium is low in this case, say around Rs. 65. If you go for an OTM put of 10,000, the premium may be still lower, may be between Rs. 30 and Rs. 40 only. This may go down even further to 1 or 2 rupees for a put of 9,500. In other words, the less is the chance for the market to go down to a particular level, the less is the premium on put".

"When the probability of NIFTY going down from 10,200 to 9,500 is almost zero, who is going to buy or sell this put of 9,500?" asked Ghisu Bhai.

"The market is full of novice and greedy investors. They keep on buying and selling low-premium calls and puts like lottery tickets. They think that they can buy a put of 9,500 at a premium of Rs. 2 for a total of just 75 × 2 = 150 rupees. If the NIFTY by chance goes down to 9,400, they would get 75 × 100 = 7,500 rupees else, they are going to lose only Rs. 150.

"Put writers like Shivlal Thekedar to exploit the feelings and greed of such investors. They keep on selling lacs of lots of OTM calls and puts at low premium to these small greedy investors and keep pocketing their money. Selling calls and puts is also referred to as call-put writing. Almost 80% of the OTM call and put options in the market expire worthless (do not reach the point from where profits may be generated) and their premiums are pocketed by call and put writers. Hence, it is also said that call-put writers are smarter than the people buying call-put options.

"However, in reality, that also is not correct, as call and put writing involves unlimited loss. If you are playing cards and you are showing your cards to the opponent, you may very well guess who is going to win. Just like those cards, your position is always visible to big traders and hence, expiries take place at the points where small investors lose money and big traders make money".

Hence, if you are a small investor, never ever after today think of getting into call and put writing. Call and put writing may result into your entire capital getting wiped out, as they have the potential for unlimited losses.

However, if you possess an appreciably high net worth and have the capacity to write a large number of call and put options at a time at different levels and manage to make money from a large number of OTM calls and puts and your set up is quite large and you are able to constantly track open positions of others and accordingly cut your positions of call and put writing, you may very well go for writing and be smart. But I know very well that a person of that calibre would not be reading this book. Hence, dear common readers, please do not make such a mistake. Please go through this book entirely and plan your trades only as per the methods and capital requirements suggested in this book.

If you still want to take up call-put writing, please do not get worried, as some subsequent chapters in this book have details of the call-put ratio spread method and also the right methods for covered call writing. You may use these methods to make profits even using call-put writing with insignificant risks. Hence, please go through the entire book patiently. I strongly believe that techniques

that I have devised are definitely going to benefit you.

I know my advice would not have still gone well into the minds of some small greedy investors having speculative attitude. They may be feeling annoyed and thinking of entering into arguments with me. But, let me explain to you how your open position getting revealed to others may harm you. This is just like the scenario discussed earlier where you were aware that supply of potato in the market was low and potato crop also was not good and potato was selling at Rs. 22 per kg in the market, and hence you were pretty sure of the market rate of potato going up to Rs. 24 per kg. Thus, you did not see any harm in going ahead with put writing for strike prices of Rs. 20, Rs. 18 or Rs. 16, as you knew that they would expire worthless. Most of the advisors also had similar opinions and your so-called charts also were showing similar candles. But, after looking at so many of your put writings, big traders like Shivlal for once and for a brief period, flood the market with potato from their own stock to the extent that the price of potato, instead of going up to Rs. 24, falls to Rs. 15 by expiry date. After realising huge profits from you people, these large traders, the moment next series starts, stop supply of potato and start buying the same from the market thereby raising the market price possibly even to the extent of Rs. 30. But by that time, all your put writings, instead of expiring worthless, wipe out a major portion of your capital.

Similarly, you should also not go on buying large quantities of call or put. Suppose you have bought in one go 1000 lots of call of Rs. 24 for potato from Shivlal. When you bought that many lots, the market rate of potato was just Rs. 22. Now, even if the supply goes down and market rate of potato is expected to go up to Rs. 26, Shivlal, being a large trader, would flood the market just before expiry with supplies from his own stock of potato to ensure that the market rate does not reach Rs. 26 by expiry date and your call of Rs. 24 expires worthless. Next day, once the new series starts, Shivlal would stop supplies and start buying potato from market resulting in rise in its market price, may be up to Rs. 28, even surpassing previous estimates of Rs. 26. But, by that time, your call has already expired worthless. This is the kind of game that large traders play and hence, small traders have to be quite vigilant while dealing in options and they should take very small positions. They should not think of call-put writing until they have big enough capital to be able to change the direction of the wind by making large trades in stocks. I had gone through a book on options by an English author where it was mentioned that the option market was structured in a way that facilitated transfer of money from the pockets of small traders to the pockets of large traders. Hence, it is better to exercise caution and take small positions only. And even after being cautioned against it, if you decide to take up call-put writing, write small lots only and apply stop loss. We will discuss this in further detail in subsequent chapters.

"So, now you have the basic information on calls and puts. Now, it's time to assign you homework. Ghisu Bhai, your homework is to make a Google search for 'NSE NIFTY Option Chain' and to view the NIFTY Option Chain on NSE website. You have to tell me tomorrow what is the premium for 'At the Money' call of 10,200 in April series. When you look at this Option Chain, you may see three kinds of premiums:

'Ask Price' meaning the premium at which somebody is offering to sell call,

'Bid Price' meaning the premium at which somebody is ready to buy the call, and

'LTP' i.e. Last Trading Price meaning the premium at which the last trade for a call for strike price 10,200 has taken place.

"So, you will search and let me know tomorrow the LTP for strike price 10,200. This is your homework".

With that, I took leave from Ghisu Bhai.

What did we learn in this chapter?

You should go through this chapter again if even after reading this chapter you are not able to answer questions like: What is a call? What is a put? What are 'Out of the Money', 'In the Money' and 'At the Money' options? What are the meanings of 'Ask Price', 'Bid Price' and 'LTP'? What is Option Chain? This is the basic knowledge that may be necessary to understand the book later.

Call-put writing should not be taken up until you have gained expertise in advanced methods like covered call or call-put ratio spread or you have sufficient margin to influence the movement of the market while writing at different levels.

□

3

Advantages and Disadvantages of Buying 'OTM' Options

When Ghisu Bhai arrived next day, my first question to him was, "What is the current LTP for call of 10,200?"

He said, "Sorry sir. I am quite busy these days. It's summer vacation time and lot of people come to parlour to enjoy ice creams. Hence, I could not get time to search on Google. Now, please you only make a search and explain to me".

This made me recollect some of the old memories of my life. I narrated the same to Ghisu Bhai. Though it is out of context, you should also definitely go through the same, as these experiences may also provide you some indications of the qualities that may be required to be a good stock trader.

I (author) worked as a teacher in Nehru Modern School in Bhadra for 3 years and 8 months during initial period of my career. I was 18 years old when, after I had cleared 12th standard in Science, my mother had refused to send me for studies any further. The reason for the same was non-availability of enough money to support my higher studies like medical (PMT, MBBS), as my father had left for the heavenly abode when I was only a child.

I had secured First Class in 12th Biology. When the manager of a large medical stores chain in the locality came to know about my proficiency in studies, he told me that he was ready to fund all the expenses for my studies right from PMT to MBBS and also to build a hospital, but with a condition that the hospital would have only his medical store for entire life.

I could sense his evil designs in no time and humbly declined his offer.

Then, I just thought about the ways to overcome my poverty and an idea struck my mind. The director of Nehru Modern School, a prominent private school in our town, was also a lecturer in Biology at the government school where I had done my 12th. He was hence aware of my proficiency in science subjects. If I requested him to engage me to teach science at his school, he might agree. I immediately went to him and after making him aware of my financial condition, requested him to engage me as a teacher in his school. I assured him that though I had not done B. Ed., I could teach well.

He was well aware of my poverty as well as my abilities. But, he got worried to see may face, as I looked like a child, not at all like a teacher.

He said, "We have two schools, first has classes from primary to 5th standard and second from 6th to 10th standard. I can offer you a job to teach only nursery, LKG and UKG classes in primary school. It will be only a half-day job, as we already have full staff. Accordingly, you will be allotted only four out of 8 periods. We pay Rs. 500 per month to teachers taking classes for the whole day and hence, you will receive only Rs. 250 per month".

I immediately accepted the offer and worked hard with complete devotion. I would teach kids A for apple, B for boy, 1,2,3,4 etc. sincerely and my head, my clothes, my hands and legs, everything would get covered with chalk powder. Other lady teachers who used to knit sweaters in their classes (there was no mobile at that time; such teachers now keep themselves busy with WhatsApp and Facebook in their classes) would laugh at me and comment, "Maheshji, howsoever you teach, you can't make these nursery kids collectors. You are unnecessarily spoiling your clothes with chalk. You should rather just pass time and ensure your payment of Rs. 250. You may just take classes like us only when you see the school directress or head mistress (who also happened to be the wife of the director of the school) coming to your side. Rest of the time you may just enjoy".

I just ignored their advices, as I wanted to move ahead and, instead of going for easy money, wanted to earn money through legitimate means. My hard work could not remain hidden from the school directors and within 15 days, they, out of their appreciation for my work, converted my part-time job to a full-time job. Thus, my salary got a 100% jump within 15 days and now I was getting Rs. 500 per month.

Within 30 days, I was promoted from primary to secondary school and again my salary was increased by 100%—from Rs. 500 to Rs. 1000 per month.

Within 2 months, they assigned me, a 12th passed student still doing B.Sc. under Open Courses of IGNOU, classes for science and mathematics for 9th and 10th standards replacing teachers already holding B.Sc. and B.Ed. qualifications. There was again a jump in my salary. Later, I completed my B.Sc. from IGNOU under their Open Courses programme.

Hence, as I had worked as a teacher for three years and eight months, I very well knew how to deal with students like Ghisu Bhai who failed to complete homework. After narrating my story, I refused to teach Ghisu Bhai any further because of his inability to honour my conditions. He said, "Sir, it does not make any difference. I just didn't get time. You are also sitting free only. Why don't you yourself open Internet and show me the NIFTY Option Chain?"

But, as a strict teacher, I didn't agree and told Ghisu Bhai that I would not teach him further until he comes back with his homework duly completed. He immediately tried to use his mobile there itself to search NSE NIFTY Option Chain, but I told him clearly, "I am not going to impart any further lesson to you even after you do this here. You will have to take time off from your social media at home and search the information relating to the LTP of April Series of NIFTY call of 10,200. You come back after memorising the same. Only then you will be entitled to further lessons".

Next day, Ghisu Bhai came with the information relating to the Last Traded Price for the NIFTY call for strike price of 10,200 as reflected in the Option Chain—it was Rs. 176. That meant, the last trade for 10,200 was made at the premium of Rs. 176 and the buyer had paid 176 × 75 = 13,200 rupees as total premium. Now, if NIFTY remains below 10,376 (10,200 + 176) until the last Thursday of the month, the buyer would not gain anything. If NIFTY closes at 10,300 at expiry, the buyer would get only 75 × 100 = 7500 rupees whereas he has already paid a premium of Rs. 13,200. He would hence incur a loss of Rs. 5700.

When I was teaching Ghisu Bhai, my wife also overheard the talks about option trading. On the basis of whatever sketchy details she had grasped, she said to me, "Hey dear, why is that we don't do option trading even though it is more profitable?"

I explained, "Look, I am a government servant. Option is a kind of trading that comes under the category of business. A government servant, as per service regulations, can't take up business while still in service".

My wife said, "No problem, I am not a government servant. I can do business".

I tried to explain to her, "Option trading is quite dangerous. Don't get into the same without understanding all aspects. You cook so well and your YouTube channel on cooking 'Seema Ki Rasoi' is also quite popular. You are also earning a good amount from advertisements on the same and you are also making small investments in stocks through cash market. If you dive into options without a proper strategy you may lose even the income you are making from 'Seema Ki Rasoi'"

My wife felt disappointed and said, "I am in any case not going to make a big investment. I also had a look at the option chain for the shares of Adani Power. The stock is trading at 32 and the lot size of Adani Power is 20,000. I will just try with Out of the Money call at premium of 5 or 10 paise".

I sensed the danger. I just acted novice and asked, "Can you tell me in detail how you are going to do that?"

She showed me option chain of Adani Power. Adani Power was then trading at 32 and its options had strike prices of 30, 32.50, 35, 37.50, 40, 42.50, 45 and 47.50. She said, "If I buy In the Money call of 30, I will be paying, at the current premium of 3.70, a total of 3.70 × 20000 = 74,000 rupees. Instead, I will take the call of 47.50 that has premium of 25 paise only. That means, only 0.25 × 20000 = 5000 rupees would be sufficient".

I asked, "How is this going to benefit? Do you believe that the stocks of Adani Power would go up from Rs. 32 to Rs. 48 by expiry?"

"No, I also know that its rate may possibly not go beyond 47.50 by expiry. But, as you said, premiums also fluctuate like stock prices and though I am not sure if its rate would touch 47.50, if the rate goes even up to 36 or 38, the premium for the call of 47.50 would rise from 25 paise to at least 50 paise and then I would earn a profit of Rs. 5000 on my investment of 20000 × 0.25 = 5000 rupees".

I then explained to her....

The premium on any stock in option trading is determined by two factors:

1. Intrinsic value
2. Time value.

Premium of an option = Intrinsic Value + Time Value.

Suppose the premium for call of 30 for the share of Adani Power that is trading currently at 32, is Rs. 3.75. In that case, out of Rs. 3.75, Rs. 2 represents its intrinsic value, as you would have got a profit Rs. 2 if it were to be settled today itself (stock is trading at Rs. 32 today). However, the actual premium is Rs. 3.75. If we reduce that intrinsic value of Rs. 2, the remaining Rs. 1.75 represents the time value. In other words, as the settlement is still 20-22 days away, market is hopeful of the price of Adani Power share going up even beyond Rs. 32 during that period and hence, that extra Rs. 1.75 that call writer is asking is actually the time value.

Similarly, the premium of 25 paise on your call of 47.50 is pure time value only. The current price of the stock is less than the strike price of 47.50 and hence, its intrinsic value is nil and the entire amount of 25 paise is only the time value. As we reach closer to the last Thursday i.e. the date of settlement, the time value would go on declining. This may reduce to even 20, 15, 10 or 5 paise only, as market now knows that the settlement is close and that rate of 47.50 is not going to be achieved.

Let's now take the case of the call of 30. Suppose the stock price goes up to Rs. 36 four trading sessions before expiry. You may observe that the premium on the call of 30 has now settled at Rs. 5.75 (this is not a fixed value; it may be any value like 5.80, 6.00 or 6.10 and the value of 5.75 has been just mentioned as an example to make things clear). What is the intrinsic value in this premium? The strike price is Rs. 30 and current market price is Rs. 36, hence obviously the intrinsic value is Rs. 6. But, how come the premium is just Rs. 5.75? Here, the time value is negative; it has gone down below zero to a value of –0.25 i.e.

Premium	=	Intrinsic Value	+	Time Value
	=	6	+	(–0.25)
	=	5.75		

This is because the market believes that there is no chance of the stock price going beyond Rs. 36; instead, during the next 4 sessions before expiry, this may even fall. That's the reason the time value has turned negative.

Try to recollect my first example where I had used Adani Power for illustration when its price was at Rs. 32 and series had started. At that time, the call of 30 had the time value of Rs. 1.75 and intrinsic value of Rs. 2, and as the time passed, the rise in stock price resulted in the intrinsic value going up from Rs. 2 to Rs. 6 and the time value going down from Rs. 1.75 to negative value of –0.25.

Had the price, instead of going up, gone down to Rs. 31.40, the intrinsic value would have reduced to 1.40. The time value might have come down to a very insignificant amount or might have even gone into negative because of the expectation of further fall in price. In other words, had the market price come down to 31.40 some 4 days before expiry, the call option of 30, that was available at a premium of 3.75 at the launch of series, would have been available at a premium of 1.40 or 1.45 only.

In short, the point is that buying an Out of the Money option is not a wise move. This is a kind of gambling and you have the risk of losing your entire premium, as there is no intrinsic value in an Out of the Money option. The premium, howsoever insignificant it may be, is entirely made of the time value that disappears by the time the option reaches expiry".

Seema said, "I have an idea in this regard".

What she told as a display of her intelligence should be carefully read by you readers also, as this fact is the fundamental principle of option trading, rather the soul of option trading.

She explained, "Look, one share of Adani Power is trading at 32. If I were to buy 20000 shares at 32, I would have required 20,000 × 32 = 6,40,000 rupees for this investment. If I buy a call of 47.50 and hold the same for a month, I would spend only Rs. 5000 as premium but in a way I would get the benefit of holding 47.50 × 20000 = 9,50,000 rupees worth of stocks.

"If the price does not reach 47.50 during the entire month, I will lose the premium of Rs. 5000. I will treat that as payment of simple interest @ 6.40% on Rs. 9.50 lacs for a month.

"Next month, I will buy that call of Rs. 47.50 again. I will keep on doing this until the price of that stock goes beyond Rs. 47.50. This may take 2-3 months and I will treat all those premiums lost as interest paid only".

I said, "You have got the soul of option trading. This may be called 'Cost of Holding'. But, this is applicable only for In the Money calls. For instance, suppose Adani Power is at 32 today and you buy In the Money call of Rs. 30 at a premium of 3.75 by paying a total of 20000 × 3.75 = 75,000 rupees. Only in that case, that Rs. 75,000 may be treated as cost of holding, as a purchase of 20000 stocks at the rate of 32 in cash market would have required an investment of Rs. 6.40 lacs whereas this could be managed with Rs. 75000 only in options.

"In the above case, if the stock were to close at 35 on expiry, you would have received 5 × 20000 = 1,00,000 rupees on account of your holding the call of 30.

"This only is the basic mantra of option trading—you get a large leverage position with small investment. (Leverage position refers to stocks acquired against borrowed money). The meaning of leverage in options is that you are able to buy a position of 20,000 shares of Adani Power by just paying a premium of Rs. 75,000, whereas you would have required Rs. 6.40 lacs to buy 20,000 shares of that company in cash market. Thus you enjoy the same position on credit for just Rs. 75,000. If there is any profit on the day of expiry on this leverage holding of Rs. 6.40 lacs, you would get the same, else you would be losing the amount paid to acquire that leverage position i.e. the premium of Rs. 75000 that is your cost of holding. You may continue to retain your holding by buying a fresh In the Money call for the same next month.

"Let me explain why the loss of premium of Rs. 75000 in the above case does not bother you much. If the stock comes down from 32 to 26 next month, you would buy In the Money call of 26. Had you bought 20000 stocks in cash at 32, this fall of 6 rupees in price from 32 to 26 would have resulted in a notional loss of Rs. 120,000 on your holding. Here, the premium of Rs. 75000 lost above is also a notional loss only, as you have already bought In the Money call of 26 afresh. Now, if the stock price goes up to 32, you would earn a profit of Rs. 120,000, thus recovering your notional loss of Rs. 75,000. Assuming that only, large investors make do with calls-puts instead of cash".

"I am also saying the same thing," said Seema.

"But this requires purchase of In the Money calls whereas you wanted to buy OTM calls. That is not cost of holding; instead, that's just gambling".

Finding Seema disappointed, I abandoned the idea of explaining this further as I myself was bullish on Adani

Power that month. I had selected Adani Power for my trading recommendations for the month on account of the breakout reflected above its 200 DMA. I also thought if Seema's gamble did work and Adani Power, going through a breakout, reached a level of 40-45, she would feel encouraged. Gradually, I would convince her that buying OTM calls and puts was detrimental to health (I mean your trading health).

What happened next???

What else could have happened? It was the same that normally happens to small investors. In fact, I had gone through a book by an English author where he had stated, "The option trading has been structured in a way that facilitated transfer of money from the pockets of small traders to the pockets of large traders". The author was right. Seema lost Rs. 20,000 that month.

You may ask how did madam lose Rs. 20,000 as she had paid only Rs. 5,000 towards premium. You are correct. Madam was supposed to lose only Rs. 5000. But, just like common small investors, madam was too confident. Along with Adani Power, she had also bought Out of the Money calls in Ashok Leyland and Bank of India at very cheap rates thinking that at least one of the three would surely go up and for the remaining one or two that did not go up, she would buy calls in the next series to carry forward her holdings.

This was the month of December 2017. By expiry, Adani Power went up from 32.40 to close at 40. Had madam avoided her greed and bought In the Money call of 30, she would have earned a profit of around Rs. 2 lacs. But, madam had the call of 47.50 and the stock traded at 35-36-37 for many days and by then the time value was lost. The premium declined from 0.25 to 0.20, 0.15, 0.10 and 0.05 only. In the end, in the absence of any buyer, the exchange stopped trading in the same around expiry and madam lost the entire premium. Same thing happened with Out of the Money calls in Ashok Leyland and Bank of India.

You may think that madam had planned to carry forward her holdings and hence, she would have bought calls of 47.50 in the next series again, and as Adani Power had reached the level of 47.50 during January 2018, madam would have recovered her loss on account of rise in the premium.

Dear readers, it is easier said than done!

Madam had lost Rs. 20,000. And as Adani Power was trading around 40.50 when new series for January 2018 was being written, the premium demanded for call of 47.50 was 0.75 and not 0.25. That meant, madam required Rs. 15,000 towards premium to buy the call of 47.50. She did not have courage for the same, as all these carry forwards including Ashok Leyland and Bank of India would have required Rs. 40000 towards premium for this month, after losing Rs. 20,000 previous month.

Madam had understood by then that it was too risky and she might lose all her earnings that way.

In fact, man never learns from other's mistakes. He learns only when he himself makes mistakes.

Now, let me explain what would have happened if, in place of Seema, it were some large investor having high net worth using options to acquire leverage positions.

On 5 December, 2017, when Adani Power was trading at 33.50, its call of 32.50 was In the Money Call option. I have already explained to you earlier that a call having strike price lower than the current market price of the underlying stock is known as an 'In the Money' call.

The case relates to 5 December 2017. That day, premium on the call of 32.50 was being quoted between 2.10 and 2.70.

In other words, if a large investor bought 20000 shares of Adani Power at 33.50 in cash market, he would have invested at least Rs. 6,70,000, but he could have bought the call of 32.50 at a premium of approximately 2.50 for Rs. 50,000 only with the same position that he would have got with his investment of Rs. 6.70 lacs. 28 December was the date of expiry for the option that month. Adani Power share had closed at Rs. 40.70 on NSE that day.

In that case, the large investor who bought the call of 32.50 would have made a profit of 40.70 – 32.50 = 8.20 rupees per share i.e. a total profit of Rs. 1,64,000 on 20,000 shares.

If the same investor, during coming months, kept on buying In the Money call options in January series, February series, March series and April series to maintain his position, he would have lost around Rs. 40,000 to Rs. 50,000 every month towards premium and thus, would have wiped out the entire profit he made in December 2017. But if the same investor, in April 2018 when the market price of Adani Power was Rs. 26, were sitting with a call of Rs. 25, he would not have in reality lost anything. Let me clarify this. Assuming he had bought 20000 shares of Adani Power in cash by spending Rs. 6.70 lacs on 5 December 2017, he would have incurred a loss of bank interest on that amount for the period from December 2017 to April 2018 i.e. Rs. 15,633 computed at the rate of 7% for Rs. 6,70,000 for four months. Additionally, as the market rate was around 25.50 in April 2018, his portfolio would have already lost value to the tune of Rs. 1,60,000. He would not have realised any profit on his holding till the time market rate remained below 33.50. But if the same investor had gone for buying In the Money calls every month, he would have earned profit every time stock price went up.

Thus, this is the basic principle of options—acquiring big position with low investment. Hope I have made the point clear that options have been structured mainly to create leverage positions with low premiums. However, Out of the Money call is not the same as taking a leverage position; that is just a kind of speculation.

We have learnt about basic principle of options in this chapter. In fact, option may also be put to another good use—as a hedging tool. Suppose you buy 7500 units of NIFTY BeES in cash market, this is equivalent to your holding of 75 NIFTY, as each NIFTY BeES ETF unit is equivalent to 1/100th of NIFTY Index value. Now, to keep your holding secured, if you buy 1 put of the lot of 75 NIFTY, it would effectively provide an insurance for your holding. In other words, if NIFTY falls, you would have earned on your put a profit of the same amount that you would have lost on your 7500 units of ETF. Thus, it is a kind of insurance and that is why, just like insurance premium, the amount that you pay to buy options is called premium. But, if you really want to earn profit by trading in this, you would have to be very cautious. To help you in this regard, several methods would be presented to you in subsequent chapters of this book; you should understand them properly and practice them with paper trades before jumping into real trades.

Ghisu Bhai was very enthusiastic with regard to options. He said, “Sir, isn’t option then is a very advanced method?”

He probably thought of option contracts as some new discovery as compared to direct buying and selling of stocks. Hence, I decided to first of all give Ghisu Bhai an account of the history of option trading. You will learn about the history of option trading in the next chapter.

What did we learn in this chapter?

1. Call is primarily used for acquiring leverage position. However, buying calls and puts without any strategy may wipe out much of your capital. Hence, you should thoroughly practise the strategies for buying calls and puts as suggested in this book and master them fully before using them.
2. Option was primarily created to facilitate creating leverage positions by spending low premiums but buying an Out of the Money call is not the same as taking a leverage position; instead, it is a kind of speculation.
3. Put is a kind of insurance for stocks held and put is primarily used as a hedging tool to secure your current position against losses.
4. There are two kinds of values included in a premium for option—one is intrinsic value and the other is time value. The time value declines with time. Thus, if you have bought call option and even if the market rate of the underlying stock does not fall, the premium of your call option would keep on declining with the expiry coming closer and hence the time value going down.

☐

4

History of Option Trading

Ghisu Bhai, like most of the people in India, thought that option trading was a very advanced method. But, that's not true. The first time option was used in this world was in Holland around 1630. That time, Dutch economy was a very powerful economy of the world.

However, around that time only, there was a mad rush among people to get rich quickly; this is known in history as Tulip Mania. During that period of madness, people were ready to buy tulip bulbs even at exorbitant prices.

Tulip plant is a much coveted decorative flower and grows from a bulb that looks like an onion. One tulip bulb grows to a beautiful flower, as you can see in the photograph below.

At that time, people were so mad about tulip bulbs that a single tulip bulb used to go through 10 to 15 consecutive trades, each with profit.

In one of the Dutch catalogue of 1637, a particular kind of tulip bulb was quoted at the price of 3000 to 4200 guilders (Guilder was the Dutch currency). Even today (as on 10 May, 2020), one Netherlands Guilder is equivalent to 42.10 Indian Rupees.

Around that time, the annual income of a skilled Dutch worker used to be 300 guilders whereas one tulip bulb was selling for 3000 to 4200 guilders. Tulips had become a status symbol among the Dutch—if there was a tulip in your flowerpot, you were treated rich, else otherwise.

It can't be that we talk of madness in tulip and there is no talk of virus with that madness!

In fact, tulip used to have a virus known as 'Mosaic Virus'. This virus only caused flame-like effects in the colours on its petals. This colour pattern used to awaken fire in the hearts of loving couples of that time. Tulips grown from seeds did not have those flame-like effects on their flowers. It used to take 6-7 years for the plant to grow from seed and have flowers, and even after that their flowers, in the absence of mosaic virus, did not have those patterns that lovers found to be like flames of fire. That's why bulbs were in great demand as they used to be infected with virus that gave the stripes on their flowers.

As the tulip bulbs were extracted during the months of June to September only, their cash or spot market would run only from June to September. By that time, the traders had discovered the process of future contract. Traders would enter into deals in advance for tulip bulbs through future forward contracts. These contracts also started getting resold at higher prices. Thus, people started buying the contract for tulip bulbs with the hope that they would be able to resell the same at some profit.

Dutch people were quite ahead in managing financial markets even in 1610. They had banned short selling in 1610 itself. Traders who entered into forward contracts for sale of tulip bulbs without holding any real stocks were in effect indulging in short selling only. As short selling was banned, such contracts were supposed to be illegal and hence they were assumed to be safe! That was because a buyer of such a contract facing loss in the deal could have simply declined to honour the deal i.e. refused to buy tulip bulbs under contract, and as the contract itself was illegal, no legal action could have been initiated against him for breach of contract under the law of Netherlands.

This madness kept on growing during the period from November 1636 to February 1637. People were buying tulip contracts assuming the same to be safe and then reselling the same with profits.

This made many people in the Netherlands too rich and the rest of the people who were yet to get rich wanted to become rich by acquiring tulip contracts.

Ghisu Bhai was thinking that he had been left behind and probably some special technique to get rich was being taught. Hence, he, in a hurry, interrupted, "What happened next?"

I laughed, "What else could have happened? It was the same that happens often with the investors in stock markets".

In the month of February 1637, there was an outbreak of an epidemic called plague in Harlem town. The fear of plague prompted people to stay indoors (similar to what we call lockdown, isolation or quarantine today). With their economy ruined, people were now disillusioned with tulip flowers. Loving couples were now more worried about plague than their love. To be able to eat and live was more important than their status symbol.

Hence, people now refused to buy tulip contracts at high prices. Buyers were missing in tulip markets. This resulted in the tulip prices crashing to the level of a simple flower, which in turn caused panic among people. Their money got blocked in tulip contracts. Finally, on 24 February, 1637, the local flower traders association got an order passed with the approval of their parliament. The order declared that all the future contracts for tulip written after 30 November, 1636 would be treated as option calls, i.e. a buyer of such a contract would have the right, if he so desires, not to buy tulip bulbs at high prices as contracted and pay in return to the call writer (who sold the contract) some percentage of the contract value (this was somewhere between 2.5% and 10%, but it can't be confirmed in the absence of relevant old data) in the form of a premium. That was the start of option market and that was when the call option came into practice.

"When did put option start then?" asked Ghisu Bhai.

Put option is just a kind of insurance wherein we pay a premium, just like insurance, to secure our cash holding against fall in price below a specific level. For instance, suppose the lot size for Reliance is 500 and its share is currently trading at 1500 and you are holding 500 Reliance shares. If you buy call of 1500 by paying some premium, you get secured for one month against any fall in price, as, in the case of a fall in price of the stocks below 1500, the put writer would compensate the difference amount.

In fact, after the emergence of option in 1637, it continued to be traded over the counter and its valuation was not based on any regulation. It was around 1900 when Put & Call Brokers And Dealers Association was established. Anybody interested in buying options would contact this firm. The firm would look for writers for the buyer and in case they were unable to find a writer, they would write the option at a specific price.

In the year 1973, Black, Merton and Scholes invented the formula for estimation of prices of options; this is called Black-Scholes formula. Computations with Black-Scholes formula may be made with the help of online calculators. This indicates, though at a higher level, whether the premium on the option is cheap or costly. This does not have any great beneficial usage in trading.

Chicago Board Options Exchange was established in April 1973. After that, right from the year 1980, New York Stock Exchange has been witnessing greater volume in options as compared to stocks in cash market. However, option has become popular in India only in the 20th century. In fact, option is now being traded in abundance as compared to the cash market.

Summary

Option was first used in the Netherlands in the year 1637.

In the United States, options became popular rapidly during the period 1973 to 1980. Since 1980, options are being traded quite prominently.

Options in India became more popular after 2001. By the year 2020, most of the investors in India also have started according priority to option trade.

In the year 1973, Black, Merton and Scholes invented the formula for estimation of prices of options; this is called Black-Scholes formula. Computations with Black-Scholes formula may be made with the help of online calculators. This indicates, though at a higher level, whether the premium on the option is cheap or costly. This does not have any great beneficial usage in trading.

This brings an end to the theoretical part of the book. By now, you have got introduced to the basic principles of option. The practical part now starts with the next chapter.

5

Ghisu Bhai's Refusal To Take Risk in Options

Ghisu Bhai was a completely new small investor. When small investors like him indulge in option trading for the first time, profit as well as loss in such trades is harmful for them.

You may laugh—how can a profit be harmful? In fact, trades of fresh investors should not earn profits. Those who earn profits in their very initial trades are never able to learn how to make money in the stock market. If they are able to make profits in their very first two trades, they assume that making money in the stock market is quite easy and there is no need to learn. And then, such traders make large investments (many times, their entire capital) in their very third and fourth trades and if, unfortunately, they lose their money in these trades, they gamble with even higher amounts next time in the hope of getting back their lost capitals.

I am purposefully writing 'gamble' instead of investment here as buying and selling stocks without giving a thought about it, without analysing company fundamentals and technicals, without looking into previous market rates, base price and net sales is gambling only.

This way, small investors who get profits in their very initial trades, quickly lose their entire savings and leave stock markets and futures and options for good.

On the other hand, if initial trades of an investor result in loss, he generally grows to be successful investor later, as he invests smaller amounts in subsequent trades and tries to learn from his mistakes. He is able to understand that investing in the stock market is an art and not a means to make easy and quick money. If that is so, should I make Ghisu Bhai lose some money?

No, I didn't mean that. No guru who teaches his student how to swim would intentionally make him drown. I just mean that when you try a new method, you should not get despaired by a loss; instead, you should treat the same as a good omen only.

OK, let me now tell you about the first trade that I asked Ghisu Bhai to make in the option market.

I explained Straddle technique to Ghisu Bhai. When you start learning how to drive a car, you should first start practising on empty lands instead of straightaway using highways for honing your driving skills. Similarly, it's good idea to learn option trading by first practising the same using Straddle technique.

What is a straddle?

When both call option and put option are bought simultaneously, it is referred to as creating a straddle. If the stock price goes up, the call earns profit and if the same falls, the put goes in profit. Thus, one trade earns profit while the other incurs loss.

Let's take an example. Suppose NIFTY is trading at 10,600 and you buy a call of 10,600 at a premium of Rs. 132 along with a put of 10,600 at the same premium of Rs. 132. Thus, you pay a total premium of 132 + 132 = 264 rupees. Assuming that NIFTY closes on expiry at 10,900, you would earn a profit of 300 points on your call. As you have spent Rs. 264 towards premium, your net profit comes to 300 – 264 = 36 rupees. If you have been reading this book from the beginning, you would be aware that NIFTY's lot size is 75. Hence, your total profit amounts to 75 × 36 = 2700 rupees. If NIFTY closes at 10,300 on expiry, your put would make a profit of 300 points resulting in a total profit of Rs. 2700. Of course, you also incur some brokerage expenses in all these transactions, but just to make the example simple, the same has been ignored. Ghisu Bhai for once got very happy and said, "Wow sir! It's really fun! This is so simple. Just buy both call and put for the same strike price and create straddle and you get the best of both worlds! You make money irrespective of the direction of market".

I just applied brakes on Ghisu Bhai's over enthusiasm and said, "Hey Ghisu Bhai, if it were so simple to make money with straddle, all the option traders would have been multimillionaires today.

"Just assume you buy call and put of 10,600 and NIFTY closes on expiry at 10,650, 10,700, 10,750, 10,800 or 10,850. What would you earn? If NIFTY falls on expiry to 10,550, 10,500, 10,450, 10,400 or 10,350, what would you earn?

"What I mean to say is that as you have spent Rs. 264 towards premium for buying your call and put together, you would not be able to make any profit if NIFTY either goes up only by 264 points or crashes by 264 points. On the contrary, you would be incurring loss only. Suppose NIFTY closes at 10,631.37 on expiry. You would get 10,631.37 – 10,600 = 31.37 rupees on your call of 10,600. Your put of 10,600 would expire worthless. You have spent Rs. 264 towards premium and you get only Rs. 31.37. In effect, you would incur loss only and on the lot of 75, this loss also would be substantial: 264 – 31.37 = 232.63 × 75 = 17,447.25 rupees. Additionally, you have to bear expenses towards brokerage and taxes. A small investor who incurs a loss of 18,000 in his very first trade would shun the market forever".

"Then what is the solution?" asked Ghisu Bhai.

"Yes, there is a solution. Let me explain to you the *'Share Genius'* technique for creating straddle in the market. This technique is quite simple.

"Following are the main points of the same:

1. Most of the options these days are weekly. However, instead of treating option position as weekly, we will assume the same to be intraday only.

2. Whenever you decide to take positions for creating straddle, just note the average price of that index (e.g. NIFTY or Bank NIFTY) for the maximum levels and minimum levels on the last 5 days. We will refer to them as SMASH (Share Genius Moving Average Series High) and SMASL (Share Genius Moving Average Series Low)".

"But I am not able to understand anything," said Ghisu Bhai.

"Don't get worried. After explaining the theory, I will assign you homework for practising the same. You will be able to understand everything then.

"3. The day you plan to take positions, look for the previous day's closing price for the stock or index for which you want to buy call or put. If the previous day's closing price for NIFTY (or the stock) is above its SMASH, we would assume the NIFTY to be in uptrend and we would buy 1 In the Money call option. If NIFTY closed previous day below its SMASL, we would buy 1 In the Money put option.

"Let's take the example of NIFTY data for April 2015 series for this. April 2015 series started on Friday, 27 March,

2015. The highest and lowest levels of NIFTY on first five days of the series were as following:

Date	Highest Level of NIFTY	Lowest Level of NIFTY
27 March, 2015	8413.20	8269.15
30 March, 2015	8504.55	8380.75
31 March, 2015	8550.45	8454.15
1 April, 2015	8603.40	8464.75
6 April, 2015	8667.55	8573.75
Total	42739.15	42142.55
Average for 5 Days	8547.83	8428.51

"NIFTY closed on 6 April, 2015 at 8659.90 that was more than the average of previous 5 days' highest levels. Hence, we would assume NIFTY to be in uptrend in this series and its probability of going up to be more. Hence, on the next day i.e. 7 April, 2015, we would buy In the Money call of 8650 of NIFTY. However, the rule for straddle technique stipulates that call or put should not be bought alone; instead, 1 call and 1 put should be bought together to ensure making profit irrespective of the trend of the market.

"4. At present, the strike prices of NIFTY have gaps of 50 points. Hence, we would buy In the Money call or put at a level based on the probability and then we would move one step up or down (100 points up or down in the case of NIFTY) and buy 1 Out of the Money call or put. As we are buying Out of the Money call or put 100 points away, this would be available cheaper than In the Money call or put.

"In the situation, our total premium for call and put taken together would be less and our chances of winning would be more. For example, here NIFTY closed at 8659.90 and hence we would buy a call of 8650; this is an In the Money call. At the same time, as a stop loss in a way, we would buy Out of the Money put of 8550, stepping down from 8650 and 8600".

Ghisu Bhai said, "But if the market remains range-bound and closes on expiry at 8600, I would lose premiums on both sides and I would be left with loss only".

I explained, "It's not like that. You don't have to wait till the last Thursday i.e. expiry of the series. You need to make a strategy to exit your positions in the straddle of call and put for one lot each the moment you realise a net profit of Rs. 500 after adjusting brokerage costs".

Ghisu Bhai said, "But how does that benefit me? If I don't get a net profit of Rs. 500 even until expiry, I would lose the entire premium and effectively I would have to bear loss only".

This is a big risk in creating straddle. Many a time, we run the risk of losing the entire premium in an attempt to earn Rs. 500 only.

The other method involves creating straddle only for intraday trade and closing positions at the end of the day with whatever profit or loss it makes. You may in this way also incur loss on some days of intraday trade, but overall chances of profit would be more as you are moving with the trend.

Ghisu Bhai did not agree to this also and said, "Sir, please tell me some method which is safer than this, if you have any".

If you are averse to taking more risk, you may use the modern form of straddle—the 4-stroke method. In this method, call and put are not bought together; instead, call and put are bought only when the market rate goes above or below a specific level. Here, the call and the put act as stop-loss to each other. I will explain this method in a subsequent chapter. Before this, let me complete the method we have been discussing above.

Let's have a look at the example afresh.

Date	Highest Level of NIFTY	Lowest Level of NIFTY
27 March, 2015	8413.20	8269.15
30 March, 2015	8504.55	8380.75
31 March, 2015	8550.45	8454.15
1 April, 2015	8603.40	8464.75
6 April, 2015	8667.55	8573.75
Total	42739.15	42142.55
Average for 5 Days	8547.83	8428.51

Had NIFTY closed on 6 April at a level lower than 8428.21, we would have done the opposite i.e. we would have bought In the Money put of 8450 and then created straddle with an Out of the Money call of 8550, 100 points above the put strike price.

A question still arises—what would we have done if NIFTY closed somewhere in between the above two, say at 8500? In that case, we would not have taken any position that day and would have waited for a clear trend of the market.

The rate of success in this method is 70%. The profit target should be set to Rs. 500 in weekly option and Rs. 2000 in monthly option. You should not aim for higher profits in straddle. Success rate of 70% means that out of 10 weeks, you would definitely reach target for 7 weeks and you may miss the same for other three weeks. In order to prevent the entire premium from getting lost, you should preferably use this method as intraday and avoid holding positions overnight. On a daily basis, you should create straddle with a target of Rs. 500 only and stop loss also for a maximum of Rs. 500. Assuming the success rate of 70%, out of 10 trades, you may earn Rs. 3500 in 7 and lose 1500 in another 3, thus making an overall profit of Rs. 2000.

In short, Ghisu Bhai, having a weak heart, did not utilise the method described in this chapter. I will in a subsequent chapter explain the 4-stroke method that he used to earn his first profit.

However, if you have the capacity to take risks and you have adequate capital, this method is successful in 70% of the cases. In this method, one call and one put are to be bought daily from Friday to Wednesday following the rules, and profits are to be booked quickly by exiting the straddle positions as and when profits become realisable by exiting that call and put. This, though, requires a lot of practice and time. You may take up paper trading for few days to practice this strategy. When you feel that you are reaching perfection, you may go ahead with live trades. I can't teach you in a book how to set a target and a stop-loss. If you read a book on car driving, you may find the same having instructions for engaging the car in gear, keeping the clutch pressed and then releasing the same and simultaneously pressing accelerator slowly, holding the steering carefully etc. Can you learn driving by reading the same only?

In fact, driving can be learnt by practice only. Similarly, even though the straddle method discussed above is sound, you would not be able have a clear conception of target and stop loss until you go through a practical exercise for the same.

If you have a large capital, you may use the above method, keeping greed and fear away, to create straddle daily and booking profit as and when the same is available.

If you have a small capital and, like Ghisu Bhai, are averse to taking risks, you should adopt 4-stroke method.

I was about to talk about 4-stroke method when Ghisu Bhai interrupted, "You have not told anything about option Greeks till now? Yesterday only, I saw a video on options created by a

YouTube guruji. He suggested learning option Greeks before taking up options. So, do you want to ruin me by making me indulge in option trading without learning Greeks?"

Ghisu Bhai had started to doubt even me. He felt that I was wasting his time by unnecessarily explaining a failed technique like straddle and that I might not know anything about Greeks etc. Just to remove his doubts, I decided to teach him Greeks and promised to take the class next day on Greeks only.

□

6

Option Greeks and Their Practical Use

It is not necessary for me to discuss option Greeks in this book. The method that I am going to explain to you in this book to enable you to make money with option trading does not have any use of option Greeks. Otherwise also, I believe that option Greeks are more theoretical and less practical.

Before writing such words for option Greeks, I apologise to the people who have got notions ingrained in their mind that their risk management is not possible without learning Greeks or options can't be used for making money without using Greeks etc. etc.

Some of those running paid courses may charge you up to Rs. 50000 to teach you Greeks. You may feel happy thinking that you have completed an advanced course and you would be able to become a multimillionaire in no time. But that knowledge of Greeks imparted by them is of no use on practical level.

It's my request to all those who are getting angry to read above lines, to please take a deep breath 2-3 times and go through this chapter in full. After that, even if you don't feel like reading this book any further or you still don't agree to my views, please do not write a negative review on this book without reading in full the last three chapters relating to planting your money tree. I have written this book keeping small investors in focus and after lot of hard work and research for 3 years. Hence, it's ok if you treat the knowledge of Greeks necessary, but please go through the book entirely and then trade using the methods suggested in this book. If even after that you feel that the knowledge that I have tried to impart is just crap, you may consider being negative while writing review for this book.

Now that the review is being discussed, let me tell you that **your 5-star review is the only *'Guru Dakshina'* to me. I don't run classes on option trading charging hefty fees. I feel content just to read comments on my YouTube channel and reviews on my books. And for earning money, instead of taking money out of my followers' pockets, I depend more on my strategies in the stock market and that is helping me earn a satisfactory income right from 2005.**

Let's take up Greeks now. There are mainly six Greeks. They are called Greeks, as they are associated with Greek or Roman words and symbols. They are as follows:

1. Delta
2. Vega
3. Theta
4. Rho
5. Lamba
6. Epsilon

All the above six are Greeks of the first order. Besides above, there are other second and third levels of Greeks like Gamma, Vanna, Charm, Vomma, Veta, Vera, Speed, Zomma, Color, Ultima, etc. Let's now go through brief details of the above Greeks.

1. Delta: This measures the rate of change in the market price of the call or put option with respect to the change in the market price of the underlying asset.

Let's understand this with a practical example. Suppose the market price of NIFTY is 12,200. You own a NIFTY call option of 12,200 at a premium of Rs. 76, i.e. you have bought call of 12,200 at a premium of Rs. 76, thus investing 76 × 75 = 5700 rupees. Now, if market price (spot price) of NIFTY goes up to 12,250, and the price of the call that you bought at 76 also rises to Rs. 109, it means that the value of your investment of Rs. 5700 also goes up to 109 × 75 = 8175 rupees and you earn a profit of 8175 – 5700 = 2475 rupees.

On the other hand, if you hold the real NIFTY i.e. NIFTY in cash (spot) market, what would be your profit when NIFTY goes up by 50 points from 12,200 to 12,250? The lot size of NIFTY is 75; hence your profit comes to 75 × 50 = 3750. That means, the profit that you got in option is less than the profit generated by the change in the price of NIFTY in cash (spot) market.

The change in the price of underlying asset i.e. NIFTY in cash market was 50 points whereas the change in the price of its call option was only 33 points (109 – 76 = 33). If computed on percentage basis, compared to the change in spot price, the premium on the option increased by just 66% of that change. In other words, if we multiply the profit in cash 3750 by 0.66, we get 3750 × 0.66 = 2475 that is the profit on premium of option. This very value of 0.66 is the Delta.

The value of Delta in the case of a call is somewhere between 0 and 1, as we saw the Delta of 0.66 in the above example. In the case of a put, the value of Delta is computed in negative. If you had put of 12,200 in the above case, its premium would have gone down on NIFTY going up in cash market. Hence, Delta for a put has value between 0 and –1.

Hope you understood that the percentage of difference in change is to be converted to 2 decimals to indicate the relevant Delta. You may consider decimal as percentage i.e. the percentage of change in the premium on call compared to the change in price in cash market is what is referred to as Delta. For instance, if Delta has the value 0.33, it indicates the Delta of a call and means that a change of Rs. 100 in cash price brings about a change of Rs. 33 only (i.e. 33%) in the premium of the call.

Now, let's understand why this entire theoretical exercise is useless for you. While computing the value of Delta, it is assumed that all other Greeks are constant whereas that is not the case in practice i.e. other Greeks do not remain constant. Thus, it is not necessary that every time NIFTY goes up by 50 points, the premium of call would rise by 33 points. Its price depends primarily on demand and supply (the number of buyers of call represents demand and the number of call writers represents supply) and the premium may go up and down based on that demand and supply. Thus, in addition to the price of the underlying asset, the premium depends on this demand and supply also. Secondly, other factors like proximity of the date of expiry also impact the price of the premium. Thus, other Greeks are never constant and hence, Delta is not a fixed value. Then, why is Delta considered so important? Why do traders in the stock market say that it's necessary to learn and understand option Greeks?

In fact, all these are hedging tools. Suppose you have taken a short position for one lot of NIFTY in futures and you want to buy a call to hedge the same. If you know the notional Delta, you may have a fair idea that just buying a call may not hedge fully your short position in futures. If there is a 50-point loss there, call would provide you only 33-point benefit and you still would be left with a risk of 17 points. This is the risk management tool and the importance of Delta is limited up to this level only. However, this also does not provide a complete risk management, as it is not definite that a particular change in the underlying asset would surely bring about the specified change in premium. In reality, the extent of impact may vary based on several other factors.

2. Vega: Vega depicts the sensitivity of the option bought by you towards market fluctuations. This means that it indicates the extent of rise or fall in your premium on 1% increase in the price of the underlying asset. In other words, it measures the percentage of change in premium of the option on account of 1% change in the price of the underlying asset. Knowledge of Vega helps you to estimate your risk i.e. you may with the help of Vega know the rate at which your call or put would move up or down when the underlying asset changes.

I will not explain complete physics related to calculation of Vega, as I believe that "गालिब ने यह कहकर तोड़ दी माला, कि गिनकर क्यों नाम लूँ उसका जो बेहिसाब देता है।".

Here, the method that I am going to explain in this book would have permission to write only covered calls or to write calls for intraday using Ratio Spread Method. I am entirely against writing naked calls and puts as the same involves unlimited risk and limited profit. When the risk is unlimited, you need to worry about or calculate that risk. The methods suggested by me would focus on writing covered calls and the same would be entirely risk-free if you follow my rules. The methods that I would discuss other than covered call writing and writing according to ratio spread method would also focus on buying calls and puts following a discipline to ensure limited risk and unlimited profit. That's the reason I don't consider learning to calculate Vega as necessary, as "गालिब ने यह कहकर तोड़ दी माला, कि गिनकर क्यों नाम लूँ उसका जो बेहिसाब देता है।"

Still, if anybody wants to learn how to calculate Vega, he may search its formula on the Internet.

3. Theta: Let me now explain the third Greek 'Theta'. Theta simply means decay in time value of an option with passage of time. In other words, the option's premium declines as the expiry approaches. This is what is called loss of Theta value. I have explained this idea earlier also in this book. For those dear readers who are used to cursory reading and have reached this point just flipping through previous pages, let me repeat that there are two factors that determine the premium for a stock in option trading viz.

1. Intrinsic value
2. Time value.

Premium of Option = Intrinsic Value + Time Value.

Time value declines as the expiry approaches, and it becomes zero on expiry. This very decay in time value is referred to as Theta.

You may ask why this has been given the name Theta instead of simply calling it loss in premium with passage of time. Well, friends, if a simple looking 5-rupee cup of tea is to be sold for Rs. 500 in a 5-star hotel, the menu doesn't mention the same as tea; instead, it has to be mentioned as **'Caffeinated Hot Beverage With Herbs Like Ginger Especially Made With Pasteurised Milk And Distilled Water (Sugar Optional)'**. Then, the same tea gets sold for Rs. 500. Thus, option is not a rocket science, but the books being sold on the pretext of teaching options and people offering courses at exorbitant fees spend their whole effort more in making you understand the **enormity of risk** than explaining **how to make profit** with options.

Its entire physics is first systematically explained with dangerous-looking Greek words like delta, vega, theta, rho, lamba, epsilon, gamma, vanna etc. and then you are told that options are not made for you as they involve lot of risks and you may lose your premium and hence you should not buy calls and puts.

You are then advised to take up call and put writing. Though this involves unlimited risk but limited profit, they assure you that they have already equipped you with risk management tools by training you on Greeks and you may jump in the fire without any fear.

And when you lose your entire capital in trades with unlimited risks, you are questioned, "Did you not compute Delta, Vega, Theta etc.? Don't you understand option Greeks? Did you not apply stop loss?"

4. Rho: It's a parameter to compare option holding against risk free interest rate. For instance, if you hold stocks valued at Rs. 7 lacs in cash and the price of the stock neither goes up nor goes down for three months, you may think that you have neither gained nor lost anything. But, in fact, that perception is not correct. Had you invested that Rs. 7 lacs in a Bank fixed deposit for 3 months, you would have earned for 90 days at current bank interest rate of 5.25% and that would have been entirely risk free. That means, if the same Rs. 7 lacs were kept in Bank FD for 3 months with interest rate 5.25% pa, the interest earned on the same would have amounted to Rs. 9187.50. Hence, if your portfolio of Rs. 7 lacs remains stagnant for three months, you have effectively lost Rs. 9187.50 towards interest income. If, instead of stocks, you buy far month (3 months) call option, the change in the premium of that call in comparison to the potential interest income of Rs. 9187.50 would be referred to as Rho.

In other words, if the premium paid for the call is less than Rs. 9187.50 and the entire premium is lost, even then the loss would be equivalent to the potential interest income, just as in the case of holding in cash. An analysis of Rho before buying call and put may provide you an idea of the same being cheap or costly as compared to the rate of interest.

5. Lamba: This parameter provides a measure of leverage. Suppose you acquire a holding of Rs. 7 lacs in cash and the price of that stock in cash goes up by Rs. 10 resulting in a profit for you. Lamba for an option with that stock as underlying asset provides you an indication of the quantum of increase in its premium that may be required to realise the same amount of profit as earned above in cash.

6. Epsilon: This is a parameter to compare option holding against dividend yield. In the case of Rho, we had compared against the interest rate. Somebody may even say that holding stocks in cash may earn him dividends whereas call does not provide that income. Hence, using Epsilon, you may compare the potential loss of dividends against call holding and assess if the premium that you are paying on the call is higher or lower compared to the same.

These were the Greeks of first order. I am not going to discuss Greeks of second and third orders in this book. Those interested in them may go through some other book on option. However, imparting you knowledge on these ideas is something similar to my teaching you how to swim through theoretical instructions on blackboards and then pushing you into a pond expecting that you would be able to swim.

You may ask, "Why then did you teach us option Greeks of the first order?" Let me explain that. For most of the unsuccessful traders, it gives them peace of mind to see other traders also losing, as they feel they are not alone. If you tell one of those losing traders that you have read the book on options written by Mahesh Kaushik and the book was great and you have learnt option trading from the same, he may get irritated and ask you, "OK, can you tell me what is Delta?" And, had I not provided you basic information on Greeks, the question would have made you look foolish and he would have then remarked, "Option is not that simple, my son! Mahesh Kaushik did not tell you about Greeks and you can't learn options without Greeks".

In this regard, you might have heard the story of a learned person. There was a learned guy who was very fond of reading books. He had read lots of books on all subjects and had acquired immense knowledge. Once, when he was crossing a river by boat, he asked the illiterate boatman whether he had read so-and-so great books on religion, spirituality, sciences etc. The boatman replied in negative. The scholar remarked, "You have wasted half of his life". The discussion was still underway when a hole appeared in the boat (there was sudden unexpected movement in the stock market).

Water through that hole started to fill the boat and make it sink (your premium started to melt or if you had sold calls and puts, your unlimited loss started to go up in an unexpected manner). The boatman asked the scholar, "Sir, can you swim?"

"I have read many books on swimming but I don't know practically how to swim," replied the scholar.

"In that case, your entire life is wasted, as this boat is about to sink!"

Hence, I am going to provide you practical course in swimming. This study on option Greeks was covered here only to make you comfortable with questions like 'Do you know option Greeks?'. People should not make comments that your knowledge of options is useless if you are not aware of option Greeks. Now you know what option Greeks are and how significant they are. Being equipped with the information on Greeks, you may now very well handle such people arguing on the subject.

□

7

4-Stroke Method for Trading in NIFTY and Bank NIFTY

Ghisu Bhai was now ready to learn the 4-stroke method to earn his first profit. This is an excellent method for trading in options in intraday. This 4-stroke method may enable you to attain a success rate of 80-90% in your option trades.

As has been explained to you earlier, there is no method that may ensure 100% success rate in trades in stock market, and if your method is providing a success rate of 80-90%, you may continue to be a winning trader.

You may create positions in options for NIFTY and Bank NIFTY using this method. If you want, you may use this method also for taking positions in call/put for any stock instead of an index.

However, **compared to a position in option for a specific stock, it is better to take position in NIFTY or Bank NIFTY, as they don't have any liquidity issues and also there is no problem of physical delivery because they get settled in cash and not by physical delivery.** In the case of a position in a specific stock, you may, despite using a right method, face problems due to lower liquidity and if you don't sell your contract before expiry, you would have to ensure availability of enough cash / stocks to take or give physical delivery.

Let's now look into the details of 4-stroke method.

Suppose, on a particular day, the close price for NIFTY Future is 10,873.30 after closure of the market. In this method, we will consider the close price not for NIFTY but for the future of the nearest expiry month for that day.

As futures expire every month, the close price for the expiry of the nearest month would be considered, though later when using options, you have to use the expiry of the nearest week.

Now, after the market is closed, you have to prepare for your trade next day based on the above close price. You have to note down on paper In the Money call and In the Money put nearest to the above close price for the nearest expiry week. Thus, if the close price of future is 10,873.30, the nearest In the Money call would be 10850 and the nearest In the Money put would be 10,900.

Next, you have to note down the high and low of trading for above call and put for the day that we are using for close price for our trade next day (you may refer to my YouTube tutorial to learn how to view historical prices for calls/puts in options).

Suppose the highest premium for the call of 10850 was 163.30 that day and the lowest was 86.45. Please note down both the values.

Next, note down the highest and the lowest premium for put for that day. Let's assume they were 175.35 and 96.40 respectively. Now you have four values (I have named this as 4-stroke method due to its dependence on four values).

Now, for the next day trade, you are ready with a chart looking like the one below.

Option Type	Strike Price	Highest Level	Lowest Level
Call	10850	163.30	86.45
Put	10900	175.35	96.40

Next day, after the market opens, keep a watch on the premium for call of 10850. The moment you find the same opening higher than the highest level of previous day i.e. 163.30 or going through a breakout above that level, buy immediately a call of 10850 and exit once you get a profit of Rs. 10. Thus, if you buy the call at 165.80, book your profit the moment it reaches 175.80. I intentionally used 165.80 instead of the previous day's high of 163.30 for above example as in the case of a breakout, the call moves up very fast and by the time you would have taken the position, the same would have definitely gone up a bit.

Incidentally, many of the brokers today have the facility to place GTT orders wherein, if you place and leave an order with a limit price of 163.50 and trigger set at 163.10, you would mostly get that order executed between 163.10 and 163.50. You may even include 10-point profit target i.e. 173.50 in such an order in advance. There is a facility to apply stop loss also in that system. For a 10-point profit target, 5-point stop loss may be too close. If you wish, you may set a stop loss of 10 points i.e. 153.10.

If, next day, that call of 10850 moves down lower than previous day's lowest level 86.46 or opens below the same, you should short the call of 10850. Here also, it's safe to keep a profit target of Rs. 10 only i.e. if you have taken short position for the call of 10850 at 85.50, you should book profit the moment it falls down to 75.50. NIFTY has a lot size of 75 and hence booking profit of Rs. 10 means you make a profit of Rs. 750.

In this 4-stroke method, a breakout from previous day's high or low enables you to make a profit of Rs. 10 within 5 to 10 minutes only.

Similarly, if the put of 10900 goes through a breakout above previous day's high of 175.35 or opens above that high, you should buy the same and exit with a profit of Rs. 10.

And, if the put of 10900 falls below previous day's low of 96.40 or opens below the same, you may go for a short position and exit with a profit of Rs. 10.

In the case of Bank NIFTY, the lot size is just 20 and hence you may keep a profit target of even 15-20 rupees as you have to cover brokerage also.

In the same way, this 4-stroke method may also be used for buying call / put for any specific stock. If you have to define your profit target in terms of percentage of the premium, you may fix the same around 5% of the premium. Suppose the previous day's high of your call was 405.60 and you buy the call at 410 after a breakout above that high, you should set your profit target at around 5% of 410 i.e. Rs. 20. Thirsting for more would not be rational, as calls and puts go down also with the same speed with which they go up.

Now the question arises what should be stop loss in this method?

A time-based stop loss, say a 5-minute stop loss, is the best in this method. Thus, if your breakout is genuine, you should get the profit of 5% or 10-15 rupees within 5 minutes. If you don't reach the target within 5 minutes, you should gather courage and exit position at the end of those 5 minutes with whatever profit or loss it is resulting into.

I am suggesting a time-based stop loss because calls and puts fluctuate quite rapidly with wide variations and hence your tight stop loss may get hit very quickly.

If target itself is only 5%, the stop loss as per rule would be half of that i.e. 2.5% only and that being too close, the same may get hit before the target is achieved. Hence, a 5-minute stop loss is a better strategy.

Before using this method in the real world, you should practice the same with imaginary trades on paper. That would provide you an idea of the kind of stop loss to be used.

Fortunately, Ghisu Bhai agreed to use this method and the very next day, he very comfortably earned his first profit of Rs. 400 in Bank NIFTY by keeping the premium of just 10000 at risk for 5 minutes, as his broker had the facility of placing GTT orders. A GTT order i.e. Good Till Trigger order has the option to set in advance a trigger to execute the order at a specific price. Even target and stop loss may be fed for the order. I only got the target set and asked him to keep a time-based stop loss and exit the position if target was not achieved within 5 minutes after activating the order. However, Ghisu Bhai was fortunate, as he reached the target of 21 points well within those 5 minutes.

Every day after that, he would keep his orders ready only for buying both call and put for NIFTY and Bank NIFTY using this method. He did not have enough margin for taking short positions i.e. writing, but people having adequate margin may earn profit on both the sides.

Thus, he started earning Rs. 400 to Rs. 700 from Bank NIFTY and NIFTY from around 80% of his trades every day. Even when he faced a loss of Rs. 2000 in 5 minutes, he would show courage and book the same. He never waited more than 5 minutes after triggering his order. If you wish, you may consider setting stop loss of 10 points.

You may practice with paper trades for few days to get an idea of the outcomes. However, its success rate is fantastic. Even if only two GTT buy orders are placed on daily basis and only 1-1 lot is used in the beginning, the time-based stop loss of 5 minutes is also not too much. If you still wish to set stop loss, a 10-point stop loss is suitable for a 20-point target. Or else, you may even keep a 10-point stop loss with a 10-point target.

But, **this is the only method where buying a naked call or put would be safe to some extent. Otherwise, you would have to plant a money tree to earn profit with a combination of ETF and covered call**; this is discussed in the next two chapters.

□

8

How To Earn Regular Monthly Income With Options

Dear readers, if you are able to comprehend this chapter properly, this single chapter may make your purchase of this book meaningful. I strongly believe you would definitely give a 5-star rating to the book after reading this important chapter.

Three years ago, I had also uploaded a video on this very subject on my YouTube channel. Those who could understand the video offered a lot of appreciation but people who could not follow the same entirely had lots of unsolved questions in their minds and I got to know many of the doubts and questions from your comments also.

OK, instead of extending this prologue further, let's get to the main story. I told Ghisu Bhai that call writing was not always bad and if he took up covered call writing wisely and prudently, that would not only be safe but the strategy would also generate a regular monthly income for him.

Not only that, many times this method may provide monthly/weekly income even without buying or selling a single stock. Ghisu Bhai was already quite excited to hear all this and hence he wanted to learn covered call first. Some of the readers may be already aware of covered calls. It's my request to them to forget everything that they have learnt about the same till now and try to read carefully the ideas that I am going to present in this regard. This would clear a lot of your misconceptions on this topic.

Many of the retired people in the United States of America are using this method for generating monthly/weekly income. You may also be quite surprised to find how many years we people in India are lagging behind in this regard.

This strategy was for the first time discussed in a research paper published in the USA during the year 1975. You may, by reading this document "*Fact and Fantasy in the use of Options*" written by Fischer Black in 1975, very well understand how successful and safe could be the strategy that is being used by investors/traders all across the world right from 1975. To use this strategy for generating monthly income from covered calls, you must first of all hold in your demat account the stock of a good blue-chip company bought in cash for a quantity equivalent to the lot size of the option of that stock.

For example, suppose you want to earn regular income by writing covered calls on the largest market cap company Reliance. The lot size of the Reliance option is 500. Thus, you must hold at least 500 shares of Reliance to be able to enjoy covered calls on the same.

There are two types of covered calls:

1. Sell-right covered call, and
2. Buy-right covered call.

1. Sell-right covered call: In this case, the option writer sells call option at strike price lower than the market price of the stocks held by him.

The followers with amateurish and obstinate attitude, due to their inability to understand this point properly, start arguing that this strategy is quite dangerous and has too much of risk. However, none of the above two strategies is dangerous.

And yes, whatever risk they have is quite low compared to the same in naked calls.

Ghisu Bhai said, "Sir, I am also not able to understand anything. Whatever you are saying is entirely beyond my capacity to understand".

I said, "Have patience. I will make everything clear to you with examples". Let's take an example. Suppose you hold 500 shares of Reliance bought in cash.

Assume that the current market price of this stock is Rs. 1400 per unit. The strike prices in Reliance option chain have gaps of Rs. 20 i.e. the options are having strike prices of 1280-1300 1320-1340 1360-1380 1400-1420 1440-1460 1480-1500 etc.

Now, if such an investor writes or sells call at Rs. 100 less than the market price of Rs. 1400, i.e. Rs. 1300 and if the premium on In the Money call of 1300 is Rs. 180, he gets a total premium of 180 × 500 = 90000 rupees.

This sell-right call has the prerequisite of holding of 500 shares. That means, once you buy shares equal to the size of a lot and hold the same, you may use that holding as a safety cover to write calls and make money every month.

In the above case, the market value of stocks held at the time of call writing was 1400 × 500 = 7 lacs of rupees. If the market price at expiry goes down to 1280, your actually incur a loss of (1400 – 1280) × 500 = 60,000 rupees on your holding. However, you have already received Rs. 90,000 as premium for the calls of 1300 sold earlier. Thus, you have actually made a profit of Rs. 30,000. Had you not gone for call writing against your stock holding, you would have incurred the loss of Rs. 60,000 on account of price drop. Call writing not only recovered your loss but also generated a profit of Rs. 30,000.

(2) Now, just think over what would have happened if the price of Reliance share had dropped to just 1100 on expiry? Even then, the call of 1300 written by you would have expired worthless and you would have received the full premium of Rs. 90,000. But this is the point where my obstinate followers argue and get angry with me and even vilify me in their comments on my YouTube video on this subject. You may ask why do they do so even though Rs. 90,000 is received. Well, they argue that the fall of Rs. 300 in the market price of Reliance stocks actually resulted in loss of 500 × 300 = 1,50,000 rupees in the value of the holding of 500 stocks whereas the amount received towards premium was only Rs. 90,000 and hence there was actually a net loss of 1,50,000 – 90,000 = 60,000 rupees.

Such intelligent followers consider it a cleverer and more prudent step to write naked calls without holding stocks in cash. As I have mentioned at the start of this book, the option market has been structured in a way that facilitates transfer of money from the pockets of small traders to the pockets of large traders. In fact, these small gullible investors indulging in naked call writing first of all do not have the capacity i.e. the capital of Rs. 7 lacs to buy and hold 500 stocks in cash. Hence, without holding stocks in cash, they go on writing naked calls just to satisfy their ego and prove themselves right and when the market goes down, consider themselves clever on getting the premium. But, just think what would have happened if the call of 1300 had been written naked charging a premium of 180 and market price of the stock had gone up to 1700? In that case, such naked call writers would have incurred a loss of Rs. 400 per stock i.e. a total loss of Rs. 2 lacs on the lot of 500 stocks. After adjusting the amount of Rs. 90,000 received towards premium, they would have incurred a net loss of Rs. 1.10 lacs.

Here, this loss is also compounded. Such a small investor becomes confident of his shrewdness once he earns a premium of Rs. 90,000 in a month, and hence, instead of one naked call, he writes 5 naked calls next month. If, fortunately, he is able to earn even 40,000 to 50,000 rupees next month, he just gets intoxicated and goes on to write 20 calls together. And then, the price rapidly moves up, stop loss fails, market opens with gap-up and with a loss of Rs. 1 lac on each lot, a total of Rs. 20 lacs for 20 lots gets wiped out.

Many a times, investors entangled in similar situations even go to the extent of committing suicide. Hence, I am dead against naked call writing. If it's a matter of writing covered calls, first thing that is worth considering is that a covered call reflects your capacity. If you hold 500 stocks (minimum for 1 lot), you have the capacity to write call for one lot only and thus you would not be able to write calls for more than one lot.

In the above case, if you wanted to write calls for 20 lots following covered call theory, you are first of all, required to hold 500 × 20 = 10,000 stocks that would have cost you Rs. 1.40 crores. Thus, if you had the capacity to buy stocks for Rs. 1.40 crores, you could have written calls for 20 lots. Had the price gone up from 1400 to 1700, you would have had to make payments at the rate of Rs. 1.10 lac per lot, totalling to Rs. 22 lacs for 20 lots. Even then, the value of your stock holding also would have gone up to Rs. 1.70 crores and you could have comfortably made the payment of Rs. 22 lacs by selling just a part of your holding.

Let's get back to the fundamental point. Our basic discussion was that if a call of 1300 for 1 lot were written at a premium of 180 backed by a holding of 500 stocks bought at the market price of 1400, and had the market price gone down by 300 to 1100, we would have incurred a loss of

500 × 300 = 1,50,000 rupees on our holding against a receipt of only Rs. 90,000 towards premium, thus resulting in a net loss of Rs. 60,000.

The answer to the same is this. First of all, if you only had a holding of 500 stocks and you had not hedged the position with call writing, you would have incurred a loss of Rs. 1.50 lacs. Thus, by writing a call, you received a premium of Rs. 90,000 and thus reduced your loss to Rs. 60,000 only. The other most important point is that the premium of Rs. 90,000 received on call writing is a realised profit whereas the loss on account of fall in market price of the stock in holding is only an imaginary loss or notional loss and this is not a real loss until you sell your stocks.

Also, you don't need to book your loss by selling your stocks at the rate of 1100. You may just pocket the premium of Rs. 90,000 and go ahead with writing the call of 1000 next month. Now you may say that if, after writing the call of 1000, the market price goes up to 1500, you would be dead i.e. you would have to pay 500 × 500 = 2,50,000 rupees.

In that case, the rate of stocks in your holding also goes up to 1500 and your total holding goes up in value by Rs. 50,000. You already have the income of Rs. 90,000 realised previous month from premium and this month also, you may have received premium of Rs. 1,00,000 towards premium on the call of 1000 written by you. Thus, you have already received a total of 50,000 + 90,000 + 1,00,000 = 2,40,000 rupees and your actual loss is Rs. 10,000 only.

Though the loss incurred in this method is less as compared to the same in naked calls, loss does take place and hence this method is not 100% safe. I do not suggest my followers to write this kind of covered calls. The other option for covered call writing is safer. Let's look into the same.

2. Buy-right covered call: In this method, the call writer writes calls above the current market price of the stock in his holding. For example, if the investor is holding 500 shares of Reliance and its market price is currently at 1400, the investor writes a call of strike price above 1400. Though 1420, 1440, 1460, 1480, 1500, 1520, 1540 are all strike prices above 1400, the investor believes that the chances of the price of stock rising from 1400 to 1500 within that month are quite remote and hence he writes a call of 1500 at a premium of Rs. 36 against his holding of 500 shares. He derives two benefits out of the same.

1. At the rate of Rs. 36 per unit, he gets total premium of 500 × 36 = 18,000 rupees. If the market price of Reliance remains between 1400 and 1500 till expiry, the buyer of the call would not exercise his right to buy the stocks at 1500 and the call writer would receive the premium amount of Rs. 18,000 without buying or selling any stock.
2. If the market rate of Reliance goes up to 1500 or 1520 by expiry and the buyer of call exercises his right to buy the stocks, the call writer would sell his stocks (bought at 1400 or even at a lower price and held by him) at the rate of 1500 or 1520 to the call buyer. This would give him a profit of 100 or 120 per stock totalling to 500 × 100 = 50,000 or 500 × 120 = 60,000 rupees. Besides that, he already has the premium of Rs. 18,000.

As all the trades in option are settled in cash in India, the call writer of a call of 1500 does not have to pay anything for the market price of 1500. If the market price goes up to 1520, he would have to pay the difference amount of 20 × 500 = 10,000 rupees. He has already received premium of

Rs. 18,000; hence he is still left with Rs. 8000 and he does not have to buy or sell any stock.

Now, let me tell you the point where I am opposed. The followers write on YouTube, "This method is quite dangerous. What if we sell a call of 1500 and the market rate of Reliance goes up to 1600? This would result in a loss of Rs. 50,000 at the rate of 1600 – 1500 = 100 per unit for a lot of 500 stocks. This method is just useless. Please don't misguide us unnecessarily".

Hey fools! You are holding 500 stocks bought at the rate of 1400. Writing a covered call of 1500 against the same makes a profit of Rs. 100 for you safe. You have paid the call buyer only the profit of Rs. 100 that you have earned by the price moving from 1500 to 1600.

Suppose the rate actually moves up to 1600. In that case, you would sell your 500 stocks (bought at 1400) at the rate of 1600 and book a profit of Rs. 1,00,000 for 500 stocks at the rate of Rs. 200 per unit. You have also got Rs. 18,000 towards premium. Out of this 1,18,000, you would pay 50,000 towards the difference in price 1600 – 1500. You are still left with net profit of 1,18,000 – 50,000 = 68,000 rupees. On this reply, they say, "But, our entire holding in stocks in sold. Hence, your statement that we may generate income every month is just bullshit. When we have already sold those 500 stocks, what we are going to do next month?"

What should I tell now? People criticise even after making a safe profit of Rs. 68,000. The pain of selling their stocks and paying Rs. 50,000 out of the gross profit of Rs. 1,18,000 to the call buyer appear to them more severe than the joy of making the profit of Rs. 68,000. Moreover, they also are worried as to how they are going to write covered call next month?

I have found a solution to that also after years of research. That's the reason it took almost three years to complete this book. Please permit me to explain the solution for above problem in the next two chapters and close this chapter here itself. Please have a look at the summary, just in case you have missed any point.

Summary:

1. Selling a call option is referred to as call writing.
2. By writing a call, you are giving its buyer, in exchange of a prescribed premium, a right to buy stocks from you at a specific price.
3. There are two kinds of covered calls: (1) Sell-right covered call wherein you sell the call for the strike price lower than the market price of the stock held by you, and (2) buy-right covered call wherein you sell call for the strike price higher than the price of the stock held by you.
4. Both the covered calls are in fact almost risk-free; still, buy-right covered call is less risky compared to the sell-right covered call.
5. Actually, there is no loss involved in a buy-right covered call. Even if you have to pay the call buyer some difference amount on account of a huge jump in the price of the stock, you may do so comfortably by selling a part of your stock holding that has already undergone increase in value after that jump in its price. However, if that sale of stocks results in your holding going below the lot size, you may be deprived of writing a covered call next month.

□

9

Unique Share Genius Formula of Call Writing and ETF, SIP

Ghisu Bhai liked my idea of 'Buy-right Covered Call' very much. He felt quite encouraged but the following two reasons made his wish collapse like a glass castle.

1. The first reason was that the method looked to be an almost impossible task for him, as he did not have enough resources. To be able to write a buy-right covered call, you need stock holding in cash at least equivalent to one option lot. The cost of one lot in cash comes to somewhere between Rs. 7 lacs and Rs. 8 lacs. Ghisu Bhai was neither having that capital of Rs. 7-8 lacs nor holding the required quantity of stocks. He was now getting the point that option market was not structured for the middle class to earn money; this was only meant for the high-net-worth investors. Ghisu Bhai was highly dejected to learn all this; I could clearly see the emotions of disappointment on his face.
2. The second reason was this. If the market price of the stock he was holding were 1400 and he sold a call of 1500 and the price went even beyond 1500 and reached 1600 on expiry, he would have had to sell some of the stocks out of his holding to pay for the

difference in price. This would have made his holding short of the lot size and he would not have been able to write a covered call next month. Hence, this was not a fool-proof system for him for generating regular income.

Hence, Ghisu Bhai said with a heavy heart, "Sir, you have unnecessarily wasted my time telling me about covered calls. Neither I have Rs. 7-8 lacs with me nor I hold that many stocks nor your system is capable of generating regular income, as the moment the quantity of stocks goes below the lot size, the system would crash".

I had already sensed Ghisu Bhai's feeling of despondency. Hence, to bring him out of the same, I said, "You don't need to worry. For this also, I have used ETF, SIP and covered calls to devise a mixed Share Genius formula that is capable of generating constant and permanent weekly income".

In this method, you have to start a monthly SIP in NIFTY BeES or Bank BeES ETF. In fact, instead of using a particular stock for covered calls, I would suggest using NIFTY or Bank NIFTY. This is because if you buy stocks of a particular company investing Rs. 7-8 lacs and if that company unfortunately sinks on account of some major change in its business model, everything would get spoiled. Hence, when it's a matter of holding stocks for Rs. 7-8 lacs, why don't we hold a combination of 50 or 30 stocks?

NIFTY contains 50 such stocks only and Bank NIFTY is also a combination of 21 stocks. Hence, out investment in an index-based ETF would be, in a way, our holding in that index in cash and then you may write covered calls in that index. Here, there is one more reason to rejoice, especially for middle class investors, as they don't need to invest Rs. 7-8 lacs for holding stocks to cover their calls.

I am writing a book separately on ETF, Mutual Funds and SIP; this is expected to get published by August 2020. If you wish to have more information on my methods for earning profits with investments in ETF, Mutual Funds and SIP, you may read that book separately later.

Let me provide you some preliminary information on this system here. In this, you have to first of all accumulate at least 9500 units of a high-volume NIFTY ETF like NIFTY BeES, Kotak NIFTY or ICICI NIFTY. The benefit of owning 9500 units is that if you continue to write covered calls and if the market goes up significantly during a month requiring you to sell some units to make payment towards your call, you would still be left with units more than the size of one lot (7500).

In this system, you have to continuously maintain one SIP in NIFTY ETF for an amount equal to 10% of your monthly income. If you have large capital, you may buy all 9500 units in one go, else you may start an SIP in that ETF for an amount equal to 10% of your monthly income and wait for the units to grow slowly to 9500. However, irrespective of whether you buy all 9500 units together or use SIP to accumulate that many units, your SIP for an amount equal to 10% of your monthly income must continue even after accumulation of those 9500 units, as even after that, profits would continue to be booked automatically through covered calls.

Every month/week, you have to write 1 covered call if your holding is 9500 units of ETF, or 2 covered calls if your holding is 19000 units, for monthly/weekly expiry for strike price at a level 5% above the current market or support price.

Now, NIFTY is never going to go up by 5% every week, as in that case NIFTY would have risen 20% every month! The same is the case for monthly expiry. NIFTY would have a growth of

60% per annum if it goes up 5% every month. Hence, out of all the cases where you have written calls at levels 5% above market price, 60% to 80% would expire worthless and you would get the entire premium and also, you wouldn't need to sell any units. If at all there is a case where NIFTY closes above 5% on expiry, your holding of 9500 units also would go up in value proportionately and you may sell the required quantity of units to book profits to recover the difference amount paid by you towards your call.

The interesting part is that even the margin that you need for writing calls may be obtained by pledging the units of ETF that you are holding.

You would have read my book 'Abdul Share Bazar Me Zero Se Hero Kaise Bana' where Abdul had said, "I currently don't trade in stocks and I make money just by trading in options". That Md. Abdul Azeez Sahab also had the same experience. After he learnt the covered call method suggested by me, he stopped buying new stocks from the cash market and as he booked profits in his existing stocks, he went on buying units in NIFTY BeES ETF using that amount. Additionally, he also started separately an SIP in NIFTY BeES ETF for an amount equal to 10% of his monthly income. Gradually, the number of accumulated units of NIFTY BeES ETF in his holding came to the level where he could write covered calls.

You may also use this formula if you want to grow fast but I have one more safe formula. You may be worried about the security of your capital because of dependence on a single ETF, as these days, even mutual fund houses are crumbling like companies. There are 18 ETFs based on NIFTY 50 in the Indian stock markets. You may select top 10 high-volume ETFs among them and then buy 950 units in each for accumulating a total of 9500 units. This would bring down your dependence on a single ETF.

Ghisu Bhai said, "Sir, this method is quite boring. I have developed a weakness for trading in the stock market on regular basis and I would not feel excited in this method. I actually want to write covered calls while also enjoying the excitement of trading".

I knew that **most of the people who call themselves investors kept losing money in the stock market with hasty trades for that kind of excitement only; they traded in the market for excitement similar to that in a cricket match.** Hence, I laughed and said, "In that case, you would have to plant a money tree. That would give you plenty of excitement".

"How do we do that?"

The process of planting that money tree will be discussed in the next chapter.

□

10

How to Plant a Money Tree & Enjoy Its Fruits Without Paying Income Tax

You might have fantasised many times about money growing on trees. In your childhood, on getting fed up with your habit of extravagant spending, your parents might have taunted you with the remark "Money does not grow on tress!" Let me tell you how to plant a tree that keeps bearing money fruits every now and then and how you may earn regular income by picking those fruits as per your requirement.

In this chapter, I am going to explain how to plant, using NIFTY ETF, a money tree that would make both your investment and your profit booking disciplined beyond your imagination.

The most significant feature of this system is that the profits booked after one year are entirely tax-free. And if your tree bears fruits before expiry of one year, even those profits booked before expiry of one year would attract nominal income tax, even lower than 0.50% as against the normal rate of 15% on short term capital gains received through profits booked within a year.

Normally, the trees that you plant get ready to bear fruits in 3 to 5 years. But, this tree of mine starts bearing fruits within a period of 1 week to 3 months. However, it's possible that you start picking its fruits only after one year to enjoy the benefit of rebates on long term capital gains.

In this method, you have to choose some high-volume NIFTY-based ETF like NIFTY BeES, SBI NIFTY ETF or Kotak NIFTY ETF.

Now, you have to first of all decide what would be your approximate monthly investment for growing your money tree. Suppose you want to invest Rs. 20,000 monthly. Divide that into four equal parts. Now, just as you invest in mutual funds through SIP, you have to invest Rs. 5000 in NIFTY BeES/ NIFTY ETF on the same day every week.

For instance, suppose you choose Friday for this auspicious work. I call this an auspicious work because, if you are able to understand the money tree and you decide to follow the same leaving all other trading activities, believe me your this decision would transform your life and you would be able to earn from the stock market a tax-free regular income that may be beyond your imagination.

Hence, having chosen Friday, you should buy any time on Friday units of NIFTY ETF for Rs. 2000, Rs. 5000, Rs. 10000 or Rs. 15000 or for an amount that you find comfortable to invest every week easily.

Now, this is up to you whether you wish to buy the same through limit order or in the open market any time. There is no need to put any pressure on your brain for the same. You may buy any time at any price on that day.

In order to ensure that the concept is properly understood by you, I will go on explaining this story of money tree using some old data simultaneously. For this, I have taken data for NIFTY BeES for the period 5 May, 2017 to 9 August, 2018. Explaining the story with practical will help you validate the veracity of the story as well as grasp its concepts easily.

5 May, 2017 was a Friday. Have a look at the price data for NIFTY BeES from 5 May, 2017 to 11 May, 2017 in the table below.

Date	Open	High	Low	Prev. Close	LTP	Close
5 May, 17	957.00	957.00	947.50	955.64	949.30	949.02
8 May, 17	955.00	955.00	949.58	949.02	950.75	950.27
9 May, 17	955.00	955.00	950.25	950.27	951.25	951.12
10 May, 17	953.00	960.70	952.51	951.12	960.70	960.03
11 May, 17	963.00	964.79	960.00	960.03	961.72	961.13

To keep things simple for you, I have assumed that you buy or sell stocks at close prices. For the people who are not aware of the difference between LTP and Close Price, let me clarify that the Close Price is the average of the prices at which trades have taken place during the last 30 minutes of the day and LTP or Last Trading Price is the price at which last trade of the day has taken place.

Thus, we will assume that we are buying stocks every Friday at the closing price i.e. at any price during the last half an hour of the market on that day. If you have Rs. 5000 to invest, you buy 5 units at the close price of 949.02 of 5 May, 2017 for a total cost of Rs. 4745.10. I have ignored brokerage, GST, STT etc. with a view to keeping our computations simple.

Now, on daily basis, we would keep a watch on the gain on our basic investment as per the market value of our stock holding based on the day's close price. Whenever we have a profit of over Rs. 1000 on our basic investment, we would book profit by selling that many stocks only that would fetch that profit amount.

"How? I didn't follow," interrupted Ghisu Bhai.

In order to understand that, please have a look at the

figures of our profit and loss on our basic investment towards 5 units, based on their market value arrived at days' close prices during the period 5 May, 2017 to 11 May, 2017 in the table below.

Date	Close	Total Stocks	Market Value at Close	Basic Investment Value	Profit / Loss
5-May-17	949.02	5	4745.10	4745.10	0
8-May-17	950.27	5	4751.35	4745.10	6.25
9-May-17	951.12	5	4755.60	4745.10	10.50
10-May-17	960.03	5	4800.15	4745.10	55.05
11-May-17	961.13	5	4805.65	4745.10	60.55

As the gain on our basic investment as on 11 May, 2017 was just Rs. 60.55, we did not book any profit because we had decided to book profit only when the gain on our basic investment exceeded Rs. 1000. Also, till that gain or loss remained below Rs. 1000, we would continue with our weekly SIP i.e. we would continue to buy every Friday units for Rs. 5000 at market price during the last 30 minutes of the market on that day.

But what is the basic condition for all this?

The basic condition is that we would neither arrive at the average price any time nor try to compute the average price. We would only focus on our basic investment value. You may keep an Excel sheet separately for the same and keep computing profit and loss on our basic investment only.

Thus, we bought NIFTY BeES for Rs. 5000 next week again. Continuing with this weekly purchase, we arrived at a position on 10 July, 2017 when we had accumulated 50 units and according to the close price of 10 July, 2017, we had a gain of Rs. 1245.70 that was more than Rs. 1000. Before we move ahead, please have a look at the position for 2 months from 12 May, 2017 to 10 July, 2017 in the table below.

Date	Close	Buy Share	Investment	Total Share	Market Value at Close	Basic Investment Value	Profit Loss
05-May-17	949.02	5	4745.10	5	4745.10	4745.10	0
08-May-17	950.27			5	4751.35	4745.10	6.25
09-May-17	951.12			5	4755.60	4745.10	10.50
10-May-17	960.03			5	4800.15	4745.10	55.05
11-May-17	961.13			5	4805.65	4745.10	60.55
12-May-17	959.47	5	4707.35	10	9594.70	9542.45	52.25
15-May-17	963.05			10	9630.50	9542.45	88.05
16-May-17	970.65			10	9706.50	9542.45	164.05
17-May-17	972.12			10	9721.20	9542.45	178.75
18-May-17	962.33			10	9623.30	9542.45	80.85
19-May-17	962.53	5	4812.65	15	14437.95	14355.10	82.85
22-May-17	963.64			15	14454.60	14355.10	99.50
23-May-17	958.01			15	14370.15	14355.10	15.05
24-May-17	955.32			15	14329.80	14355.10	–25.30
25-May-17	970.46			15	14556.90	14355.10	201.80
26-May-17	978.89	5	4894.45	20	19577.80	19249.55	328.25
29-May-17	980.29			20	19605.80	19249.55	356.25

Date	Close	Buy Share	Investment	Total Share	Market Value at Close	Basic Investment Value	Profit Loss
30-May-17	981.75			20	19635.00	19249.55	385.45
31-May-17	982.22			20	19644.40	19249.55	394.85
01-Jun-17	980.07			20	19641.40	19249.55	391.85
02-Jun-17	986.33	5	4931.65	25	24658.25	24181.20	477.05
05-Jun-17	989.44			25	24736.00	24181.20	554.80
06-Jun-17	985.50			25	24637.50	24181.20	456.30
07-Jun-17	987.78			25	24694.50	24181.20	513.30
08-Jun-17	987.38			25	24684.50	24181.20	503.30
09-Jun-17	989.54	5	4947.70	30	29686.20	29128.90	557.30
12-Jun-17	983.25			30	29497.50	29128.90	368.60
13-Jun-17	984.24			30	29527.20	29128.90	398.30
14-Jun-17	983.71			30	29511.30	29128.90	382.40
15-Jun-17	980.40			30	29412.00	29128.90	283.10
16-Jun-17	980.52	5	4902.60	35	34318.20	34031.50	286.70
19-Jun-17	988.26			35	34589.10	34031.50	557.60
20-Jun-17	988.77			35	34606.95	34031.50	575.45
21-Jun-17	985.75			35	34501.25	34031.50	469.75

Date	Close	Buy Share	Investment	Total Share	Market Value at Close	Basic Investment Value	Profit Loss
22-Jun-17	985.00			35	34475.00	34031.50	443.50
23-Jun-17	980.29	5	4901.45	40	39211.60	38932.95	278.65
27-Jun-17	973.47			40	38938.80	38932.95	5.85
28-Jun-17	972.68			40	38907.20	38932.95	-25.75
29-Jun-17	973.55			40	38942.00	38932.95	9.05
30-Jun-17	975.98	5	4879.90	45	43919.10	43812.85	106.25
03-Jul-17	984.21			45	44289.44	43812.85	476.60
04-Jul-17	985.08			45	44328.60	43812.85	515.75
05-Jul-17	987.86			45	44453.70	43812.85	640.85
06-Jul-17	992.07			45	44643.15	43812.85	830.30
07-Jul-17	990.09	5	4950.45	50	49504.50	48763.30	741.20
10-Jul-17	1000.18			50	50009.00	48763.30	1245.70

You can see that we had net profit of Rs. 1245.70 on our basic investment amount as on 10 July, 2017. Now, we have to take this profit of Rs. 1245.70 out of the market. For this, we sell 1 unit next day i.e. 11 July, 2017 by placing a limit order with close price Rs. 1008.18 of 10 July, 2017. We decided to sell only 1 unit, as selling two units would have resulted in booking profit for an amount greater than Rs. 1245.70.

Thus, we have taken out Rs. 1008.18 treating the same as our profit only. In other words, we have picked the first fruit from our tree.

We are now left with 49 units. The basic investment that we made for buying 50 units was Rs. 48763.30. This basic investment is not to be reduced and we have to assume that our basic investment is intact and we have withdrawn Rs. 1008.18 from profit only. In other words, we have just picked a fruit and our tree is intact.

Hence, while computing the next profit exceeding Rs. 1000, we have to treat our basic investment as Rs. 48763.30 only and as and when we buy new units, related investment amount would be added to this basic investment and profit of Rs. 1000 and above would be computed for that total investment.

But what is the benefit of doing that?

Firstly, we only know that we have withdrawn Rs. 1008.18 as profit, that also within a period of just 2 months and 5 days, but as per Income Tax regulations, this is not your profit. You have just sold 1 share that was bought at an average price of Rs. 975.26, for Rs. 1008.18, and as per Income Tax regulations, you have booked a profit of Rs. 32.92 only. If you adjust around Rs. 20 towards brokerage, STT, GST, delivery charge etc., you are left with only 13 rupees as profit. The short-term capital gains tax on the same @15% would come to Rs. 1.95 only. Thus, you would have to pay just Rs. 1.95 as income tax on the profit of Rs. 1008.18, effectively coming to 0.20% approximately. Similarly, if you sell any share after this tree gets more than a year old, the same would be treated as the one bought a year back and accordingly, such profits, to be treated as long term capital gains, up to an amount of Rs. 1 lac per year would not attract any income tax.

Now, please have a look at the data for entire 15 months to notice when and how only limited quantities of shares were sold to book profits, ensuring that the basic investment amount remained invested in the market.

Date	Close	Buy Share	Investment	Total Share	Market Value at Close	Basic Investment Value	Profit/ Loss
05-May-17	949.02	5	4745.1	5	4745.1	4745.1	0
08-May-17	950.27			5	4751.35	4745.1	6.25
09-May-17	951.12			5	4755.6	4745.1	10.5
10-May-17	960.03			5	4800.15	4745.1	55.05
11-May-17	961.13			5	4805.65	4745.1	60.55
12-May-17	959.47	5	4797.35	10	9594.7	9542.45	52.25
15-May-17	963.05			10	9630.5	9542.45	88.05
16-May-17	970.65			10	9706.5	9542.45	164.05
17-May-17	972.12			10	9721.2	9542.45	178.75
18-May-17	962.33			10	9623.3	9542.45	80.85
19-May-17	962.53	5	4812.65	15	14437.95	14355.1	82.85
22-May-17	963.64			15	14454.6	14355.1	99.5
23-May-17	958.01			15	14370.15	14355.1	15.05
24-May-17	955.32			15	14329.8	14355.1	–25.3
25-May-17	970.46			15	14556.9	14355.1	201.8
26-May-17	978.89	5	4894.45	20	19577.8	19249.55	328.25
29-May-17	980.29			20	19605.8	19249.55	356.25

Date	Close	Buy Share	Investment	Total Share	Market Value at Close	Basic Investment Value	Profit/ Loss
30-May-17	981.75			20	19635	19249.55	385.45
31-May-17	982.22			20	19644.4	19249.55	394.85
01-Jun-17	982.07			20	19641.4	19249.55	391.85
02-Jun-17	986.33	5	4931.65	25	24658.25	24181.2	477.05
05-Jun-17	989.44			25	24736	24181.2	554.8
06-Jun-17	985.5			25	24637.5	24181.2	456.3
07-Jun-17	987.78			25	24694.5	24181.2	513.3
08-Jun-17	987.38			25	24684.5	24181.2	503.3
09-Jun-17	989.54	5	4947.7	30	29686.2	29128.9	557.3
12-Jun-17	983.25			30	29497.5	29128.9	368.6
13-Jun-17	984.24			30	29527.2	29128.9	398.3
14-Jun-17	983.71			30	29511.3	29128.9	382.4
15-Jun-17	980.4			30	29412	29128.9	283.1
16-Jun-17	980.52	5	4902.6	35	34318.2	34031.5	286.7
19-Jun-17	988.26			35	34589.1	34031.5	557.6
20-Jun-17	988.77			35	34606.95	34031.5	575.45

Date	Close	Buy Share	Investment	Total Share	Market Value at Close	Basic Investment Value	Profit/ Loss
21-Jun-17	985.75			35	34501.25	34031.5	469.75
22-Jun-17	985			35	34475	34031.5	443.5
23-Jun-17	980.29	5	4901.45	40	39211.6	38932.95	278.65
27-Jun-17	973.47			40	38938.8	38932.95	5.85
28-Jun-17	972.68			40	38907.2	38932.95	–25.75
29-Jun-17	973.55			40	38942	38932.95	9.05
30-Jun-17	975.98	5	4879.9	45	43919.1	43812.85	106.25
03-Jul-17	984.21			45	44289.45	43812.85	476.6
04-Jul-17	985.08			45	44328.6	43812.85	515.75
05-Jul-17	987.86			45	44453.7	43812.85	640.85
06-Jul-17	992.07			45	44643.15	43812.85	830.3
07-Jul-17	990.09	5	4950.45	50	49504.5	48763.3	741.2
10-Jul-17	1,000.18			50	50009	48763.3	1245.7
Next Day Sell Quantity						1	
Estimated Profit Taking						1008.18	
11-Jul-17	1,003.84			49	49188.16	48763.3	424.86
12-Jul-17	1,005.54			49	49271.46	48763.3	508.16

Date	Close	Buy Share	Investment	Total Share	Market Value at Close	Basic Investment Value	Profit/ Loss
13-Jul-17	1,014.25			49	49698.25	48763.3	934.95
14-Jul-17	1,012.44	5	5062.2	54	54671.76	53825.5	846.26
17-Jul-17	1,016.88			54	54911.52	53825.5	1086
Next Day Sell Quantity						Nil	
Estimated Profit Taking						**0**	
Profit booking 0 because next day ETF traded below last close price, so unable to sell. I think honesty is the best policy							
18-Jul-17	1,010.11			54	54545.94	53825.5	720.44
19-Jul-17	1,016.32			54	54881.28	53825.5	1055.8
Next Day Sell Quantity						1	
Estimated Profit Taking						1016.32	
20-Jul-17	1,014.73			53	53780.69	53825.5	–44.81
21-Jul-17	1,017.73	5	5088.65	58	59028.34	58914.15	114.19
24-Jul-17	1,023.86			58	59383.88	58914.15	469.73
25-Jul-17	1,024.98			58	59448.84	58914.15	534.69
26-Jul-17	1,028.62			58	59659.96	58914.15	745.81
27-Jul-17	1,030.46			58	59766.68	58914.15	852.53

Date	Close	Buy Share	Investment	Total Share	Market Value at Close	Basic Investment Value	Profit/ Loss
28-Jul-17	1,027.57	5	5137.85	63	64736.91	64052	684.91
31-Jul-17	1,034.27			63	65159.01	64052	1107
Next Day Sell Quantity					1		
Estimated Profit Taking					1034.27		
01-Aug-17	1,037.39			62	64318.18	64052	266.18
02-Aug-17	1,037.78			62	64342.36	64052	290.36
03-Aug-17	1,030.69			62	63902.78	64052	-149.2
04-Aug-17	1,037.47	5	5187.35	67	69510.49	69239.35	271.14
07-Aug-17	1,035.00			67	69345	69239.35	105.65
08-Aug-17	1,029.12			67	68951.04	69239.35	-288.3
09-Aug-17	1,020.77			67	68391.59	69239.35	-847.8
10-Aug-17	1,006.75			67	67452.25	69239.35	-1787
11-Aug-17	997.78	5	4988.9	72	71840.16	74228.25	-2388
14-Aug-17	1,009.35			72	72673.2	74228.25	-1555
16-Aug-17	1,020.84			72	73500.48	74228.25	-727.8
17-Aug-17	1,021.60			72	73555.2	74228.25	-673.1
18-Aug-17	1,016.08	5	5080.4	77	78238.16	79308.65	-1070

Date	Close	Buy Share	Investment	Total Share	Market Value at Close	Basic Investment Value	Profit/ Loss
21-Aug-17	1,005.97			77	77459.69	79308.65	-1849
22-Aug-17	1,007.49			77	77576.73	79308.65	-1732
23-Aug-17	1,015.31			77	78178.87	79308.65	-1130
24-Aug-17	1,017.59			77	78354.43	79308.65	-954.2
28-Aug-17	1,022.78	5	5113.9	82	83867.96	84422.55	-554.6
29-Aug-17	1,010.69			82	82876.58	84422.55	-1546
30-Aug-17	1,018.74			82	83536.68	84422.55	-885.9
31-Aug-17	1,021.53			82	83765.46	84422.55	-657.1
01-Sep-17	1,028.56	5	5142.8	87	89484.72	89565.35	-80.63
04-Sep-17	1,020.68			87	88799.16	89565.35	-766.2
05-Sep-17	1,024.59			87	89139.33	89565.35	-426
06-Sep-17	1,021.33			87	88855.71	89565.35	-709.6
07-Sep-17	1,023.52			87	89046.24	89565.35	-519.1
08-Sep-17	1,022.80	5	5114	92	94097.6	94679.35	-581.8
11-Sep-17	1,030.52			92	94807.84	94679.35	128.49
12-Sep-17	1,037.56			92	95455.52	94679.35	776.17
13-Sep-17	1,035.99			92	95311.08	94679.35	631.73

Date	Close	Buy Share	Investment	Total Share	Market Value at Close	Basic Investment Value	Profit/ Loss
14-Sep-17	1,037.64			92	95462.88	94679.35	783.53
15-Sep-17	1,037.57	5	5187.85	97	100644.3	99867.2	777.09
18-Sep-17	1,045.13			97	101377.6	99867.2	1510.4
Next Day Sell Quantity					1		
Estimated Profit Taking					1045.13		
19-Sep-17	1,044.72			96	100293.1	99867.2	425.92
20-Sep-17	1,044.38			96	100260.5	99867.2	393.28
21-Sep-17	1,040.09			96	99848.64	99867.2	-18.56
22-Sep-17	1,025.53	5	5127.65	101	103578.5	104994.9	-1416
25-Sep-17	1,016.95			101	102712	104994.9	-2283
26-Sep-17	1,013.93			101	102406.9	104994.9	-2588
27-Sep-17	1,006.22			101	101628.2	104994.9	-3367
28-Sep-17	1,010.05			101	102015.1	104994.9	-2980
29-Sep-17	1,009.98	5	5049.9	106	107057.9	110044.8	-2987
03-Oct-17	1,015.03			106	107593.2	110044.8	-2452
04-Oct-17	1,020.69			106	108193.1	110044.8	-1852
05-Oct-17	1,018.65			106	107976.9	110044.8	-2068

Date	Close	Buy Share	Investment	Total Share	Market Value at Close	Basic Investment Value	Profit/ Loss
06-Oct-17	1,030.78	5	5153.9	111	114416.6	115198.7	-782.1
09-Oct-17	1,030.84			111	114423.2	115198.7	-775.4
10-Oct-17	1,032.04			111	114556.4	115198.7	-642.2
11-Oct-17	1,027.71			111	114075.8	115198.7	-1123
12-Oct-17	1,038.68			111	115293.5	115198.7	94.83
13-Oct-17	1,049.73	5	5248.65	116	121768.7	120447.3	1321.4
Next Day Sell Quantity						1	
Estimated Profit Taking						1049.73	
16-Oct-17	1,055.96			115	121435.4	120447.3	988.1
17-Oct-17	1,055.37			115	121367.6	120447.3	920.25
18-Oct-17	1,053.95			115	121204.3	120447.3	756.95
19-Oct-17	1,046.98			115	120402.7	120447.3	-44.6
23-Oct-17	1,051.64	5	5258.2	120	126196.8	125705.5	491.3
24-Oct-17	1,049.27			120	125912.4	125705.5	206.9
25-Oct-17	1,059.48			120	127137.6	125705.5	1432.1

Date	Close	Buy Share	Investment	Total Share	Market Value at Close	Basic Investment Value	Profit/ Loss
Next Day Sell Quantity					1		
Estimated Profit Taking					1059.48		
26-Oct-17	1,063.81			119	126593.4	125705.5	887.89
27-Oct-17	1,062.02	5	5310.1	124	131690.5	131015.6	674.88
30-Oct-17	1,069.49			124	132616.8	131015.6	1601.2
Next Day Sell Quantity					1		
Estimated Profit Taking					1069.49		
31-Oct-17	1,065.17			123	131015.9	131015.6	0.31
01-Nov-17	1,074.61			123	132177	131015.6	1161.4
Next Day Sell Quantity					1		
Estimated Profit Taking					1074.61		
02-Nov-17	1,074.33			122	131068.3	131015.6	52.66
03-Nov-17	1,076.66	5	5383.3	127	136735.8	136398.9	336.92
06-Nov-17	1,076.69			127	136739.6	136398.9	340.73
07-Nov-17	1,068.62			127	135714.7	136398.9	-684.2
08-Nov-17	1,063.09			127	135012.4	136398.9	-1386
09-Nov-17	1,061.56			127	134818.1	136398.9	-1581

Date	Close	Buy Share	Investment	Total Share	Market Value at Close	Basic Investment Value	Profit/ Loss
10-Nov-17	1,062.61	5	5313.05	132	140264.5	141712	-1447
13-Nov-17	1,056.08			132	139402.6	141712	-2309
14-Nov-17	1,052.04			132	138869.3	141712	-2843
15-Nov-17	1,044.66			132	137895.1	141712	-3817
16-Nov-17	1,052.29			132	138902.3	141712	-2810
17-Nov-17	1,058.92	5	5294.6	137	145072	147006.6	-1935
20-Nov-17	1,061.83			137	145470.7	147006.6	-1536
21-Nov-17	1,063.83			137	145744.7	147006.6	-1262
22-Nov-17	1,064.62			137	145852.9	147006.6	-1154
23-Nov-17	1,065.81			137	146016	147006.6	-990.6
24-Nov-17	1,069.46	5	5347.3	142	151863.3	152353.9	-490.5
27-Nov-17	1,069.85			142	151918.7	152353.9	-435.1
28-Nov-17	1,068.41			142	151714.2	152353.9	-639.6
29-Nov-17	1,067.82			142	151630.4	152353.9	-723.4
30-Nov-17	1,057.46			142	150159.3	152353.9	-2195
01-Dec-17	1,046.15	5	5230.75	147	153784.1	157584.6	-3801

Date	Close	Buy Share	Investment	Total Share	Market Value at Close	Basic Investment Value	Profit/ Loss
04-Dec-17	1,046.95			147	153901.7	157584.6	-3683
05-Dec-17	1,046.00			147	153762	157584.6	-3823
06-Dec-17	1,037.72			147	152544.8	157584.6	-5040
07-Dec-17	1,051.06			147	154505.8	157584.6	-3079
08-Dec-17	1,060.46	5	5302.3	152	161189.9	162886.9	-1697
11-Dec-17	1,062.93			152	161565.4	162886.9	-1322
12-Dec-17	1,055.98			152	160509	162886.9	-2378
13-Dec-17	1,052.07			152	159914.6	162886.9	-2972
14-Dec-17	1,054.02			152	160211	162886.9	-2676
15-Dec-17	1,063.71	5	5318.55	157	167002.5	168205.5	-1203
18-Dec-17	1,069.26			157	167873.8	168205.5	-331.6
19-Dec-17	1,077.82			157	169217.7	168205.5	1012.3
Next Day Sell Quantity					1		
Estimated Profit Taking					1077.82		
20-Dec-17	1,075.13			156	167720.3	168205.5	-485.2
21-Dec-17	1,074.49			156	167620.4	168205.5	-585

Date	Close	Buy Share	Investment	Total Share	Market Value at Close	Basic Investment Value	Profit/ Loss
22-Dec-17	1,079.36	5	5396.8	161	173777	173602.3	174.71
26-Dec-17	1,082.81			161	174332.4	173602.3	730.16
27-Dec-17	1,082.37			161	174261.6	173602.3	659.32
28-Dec-17	1,079.88			161	173860.7	173602.3	258.43
29-Dec-17	1,084.48	5	5422.4	166	180023.7	179024.7	999.03
01-Jan-18	1,078.14			166	178971.2	179024.7	-53.41
02-Jan-18	1,074.61			166	178385.3	179024.7	-639.4
03-Jan-18	1,076.29			166	178664.1	179024.7	-360.5
04-Jan-18	1,081.76			166	179572.2	179024.7	547.51
05-Jan-18	1,087.20	5	5436	171	185911.2	184460.7	1450.6
Next Day Sell Quantity						1	
Estimated Profit Taking						1087.20	
08-Jan-18	1,092.46			170	185718.2	184460.7	1257.6
Next Day Sell Quantity						1	
Estimated Profit Taking						1092.46	
09-Jan-18	1,094.91			169	185039.8	184460.7	579.14
10-Jan-18	1,099.07			169	185742.8	184460.7	1282.2

Date	Close	Buy Share	Investment	Total Share	Market Value at Close	Basic Investment Value	Profit/ Loss
Next Day Sell Quantity					1		
Estimated Profit Taking					1099.07		
11-Jan-18	1,100.29			168	184848.7	184460.7	388.07
12-Jan-18	1,102.69	5	5513.45	173	190765.4	189974.1	791.27
15-Jan-18	1,109.02			173	191860.5	189974.1	1886.4
Next Day Sell Quantity					1		
Estimated Profit Taking					1109.02		
16-Jan-18	1,103.79			172	189851.9	189974.1	-122.2
17-Jan-18	1,110.49			172	191004.3	189974.1	1030.2
Next Day Sell Quantity					1		
Estimated Profit Taking					1110.49		
18-Jan-18	1,115.38			171	190730	189974.1	755.88
19-Jan-18	1,121.84	4	4487.36	175	196322	194461.5	1860.5
Next Day Sell Quantity					1		
Estimated Profit Taking					1121.84		
22-Jan-18	1,128.79			174	196409.5	194461.5	1948

Date	Close	Buy Share	Investment	Total Share	Market Value at Close	Basic Investment Value	Profit/ Loss
Next Day Sell Quantity						1	
Estimated Profit Taking						1128.79	
23-Jan-18	1,141.89			173	197547	194461.5	3085.5
Next Day Sell Quantity						3	
Estimated Profit Taking						3425.67	
24-Jan-18	1,141.95			170	194131.5	194461.5	-330
25-Jan-18	1,139.31			170	193682.7	194461.5	-778.8
29-Jan-18	1,146.27	4	4585.08	174	199451	199046.5	404.44
30-Jan-18	1,137.14			174	197862.4	199046.5	-1184
31-Jan-18	1,135.44			174	197566.6	199046.5	-1480
01-Feb-18	1,135.03			174	197495.2	199046.5	-1551
02-Feb-18	1,112.49	4	4449.96	178	198023.2	203496.5	-5473
05-Feb-18	1,102.94			178	196323.3	203496.5	-7173
06-Feb-18	1,087.35			178	193548.3	203496.5	-9948
07-Feb-18	1,083.85			178	192925.3	203496.5	-10571
08-Feb-18	1,094.94			178	194899.3	203496.5	-8597

Date	Close	Buy Share	Investment	Total Share	Market Value at Close	Basic Investment Value	Profit/ Loss
09-Feb-18	1,082.32	5	5411.6	183	198064.6	208908.1	-10844
12-Feb-18	1,091.35			183	199717.1	208908.1	-9191
14-Feb-18	1,086.53			183	198835	208908.1	-10073
15-Feb-18	1,092.15			183	199863.5	208908.1	-9045
16-Feb-18	1,082.69	5	5413.45	188	203545.7	214321.6	-10776
19-Feb-18	1,074.10			188	201930.8	214321.6	-12391
20-Feb-18	1,071.76			188	201490.9	214321.6	-12831
21-Feb-18	1,076.56			188	202393.3	214321.6	-11928
22-Feb-18	1,074.63			188	202030.4	214321.6	-12291
23-Feb-18	1,084.68	5	5423.4	193	209343.2	219745	-10402
26-Feb-18	1,093.56			193	211057.1	219745	-8688
27-Feb-18	1,089.94			193	210358.4	219745	-9387
28-Feb-18	1,086.70			193	209733.1	219745	-10012
01-Mar-18	1,081.19			193	208669.7	219745	-11075
05-Mar-18	1,071.74	5	5358.7	198	212204.5	225103.7	-12899
06-Mar-18	1,060.94			198	210066.1	225103.7	-15038

Date	Close	Buy Share	Investment	Total Share	Market Value at Close	Basic Investment Value	Profit/ Loss
07-Mar-18	1,050.67			198	208032.7	225103.7	–17071
08-Mar-18	1,059.59			198	209798.8	225103.7	–15305
09-Mar-18	1,059.04	5	5295.2	203	214985.1	230398.9	–15414
12-Mar-18	1,079.89			203	219217.7	230398.9	–11181
13-Mar-18	1,079.15			203	219067.5	230398.9	–11331
14-Mar-18	1,078.19			203	218872.6	230398.9	–11526
15-Mar-18	1,072.57			203	217731.7	230398.9	–12667
16-Mar-18	1,056.78	5	5283.9	208	219810.2	235682.8	–15873
19-Mar-18	1,047.70			208	217921.6	235682.8	–17761
20-Mar-18	1,046.47			208	217665.8	235682.8	–18017
21-Mar-18	1,049.05			208	218202.4	235682.8	–17480
22-Mar-18	1,045.79			208	217524.3	235682.8	–18158
23-Mar-18	1,036.78	5	5183.9	213	220834.1	240866.7	–20033
26-Mar-18	1,047.05			213	223021.7	240866.7	–17845
27-Mar-18	1,051.84			213	224041.9	240866.7	–16825
28-Mar-18	1,049.25			213	223490.3	240866.7	–17376

Date	Close	Buy Share	Investment	Total Share	Market Value at Close	Basic Investment Value	Profit/ Loss
02-Apr-18	1,058.12	5	5290.6	218	230670.2	246157.3	-15487
03-Apr-18	1,062.70			218	231668.6	246157.3	-14489
04-Apr-18	1,049.52			218	228795.4	246157.3	-17362
05-Apr-18	1,069.01			218	233044.2	246157.3	-13113
06-Apr-18	1,068.69	5	5343.45	223	238317.9	251500.7	-13183
09-Apr-18	1,073.58			223	239408.3	251500.7	-12092
10-Apr-18	1,076.05			223	239959.2	251500.7	-11542
11-Apr-18	1,078.44			223	240492.1	251500.7	-11009
12-Apr-18	1,084.00			223	241732	251500.7	-9769
13-Apr-18	1,084.75	5	5423.75	228	247323	256924.5	-9601
16-Apr-18	1,089.37			228	248376.4	256924.5	-8548
17-Apr-18	1,089.11			228	248317.1	256924.5	-8607
18-Apr-18	1,086.80			228	247790.4	256924.5	-9134
19-Apr-18	1,091.52			228	248866.6	256924.5	-8058
20-Apr-18	1,090.04	5	5450.2	233	253979.3	262374.7	-8395
23-Apr-18	1,094.72			233	255069.8	262374.7	-7305

Date	Close	Buy Share	Investment	Total Share	Market Value at Close	Basic Investment Value	Profit/ Loss
24-Apr-18	1,097.75			233	255775.8	262374.7	-6599
25-Apr-18	1,092.79			233	254620.1	262374.7	-7755
26-Apr-18	1,098.59			233	255971.5	262374.7	-6403
27-Apr-18	1,105.53	5	5527.65	238	263116.1	267902.3	-4786
30-Apr-18	1,111.68			238	264579.8	267902.3	-3322
02-May-18	1,107.71			238	263635	267902.3	-4267
03-May-18	1,105.29			238	263059	267902.3	-4843
04-May-18	1,100.19	5	5500.95	243	267346.2	273403.3	-6057
07-May-18	1,107.22			243	269054.5	273403.3	-4349
08-May-18	1,108.38			243	269336.3	273403.3	-4067
09-May-18	1,112.23			243	270271.9	273403.3	-3131
10-May-18	1,107.94			243	269229.4	273403.3	-4174
11-May-18	1,116.06	4	4464.24	247	275666.8	277867.5	-2201
14-May-18	1,116.89			247	275871.8	277867.5	-1996
15-May-18	1,117.17			247	275941	277867.5	-1926
16-May-18	1,111.93			247	274646.7	277867.5	-3221

Date	Close	Buy Share	Investment	Total Share	Market Value at Close	Basic Investment Value	Profit/ Loss
17-May-18	1,106.31			247	273258.6	277867.5	-4609
18-May-18	1,096.05	5	5480.25	252	276204.6	283347.7	-7143
21-May-18	1,090.49			252	274803.5	283347.7	-8544
22-May-18	1,092.81			252	275388.1	283347.7	-7960
23-May-18	1,078.64			252	271817.3	283347.7	-11530
24-May-18	1,085.42			252	273525.8	283347.7	-9822
25-May-18	1,098.11	5	5490.55	257	282214.3	288838.3	-6624
28-May-18	1,110.51			257	285401.1	288838.3	-3437
29-May-18	1,103.69			257	283648.3	288838.3	-5190
30-May-18	1,102.99			257	283468.4	288838.3	-5370
31-May-18	1,112.50			257	285912.5	288838.3	-2926
01-Jun-18	1,109.92	5	5549.6	262	290799	294387.9	-3589
04-Jun-18	1,101.16			262	288503.9	294387.9	-5884
05-Jun-18	1,101.85			262	288684.7	294387.9	-5703
06-Jun-18	1,109.96			262	290809.5	294387.9	-3578
07-Jun-18	1,117.89			262	292887.2	294387.9	-1501

Date	Close	Buy Share	Investment	Total Share	Market Value at Close	Basic Investment Value	Profit/ Loss
08-Jun-18	1,118.52	4	4474.08	266	297526.3	298862	-1336
11-Jun-18	1,122.52			266	298590.3	298862	-271.6
12-Jun-18	1,126.27			266	299587.8	298862	725.85
13-Jun-18	1,125.66			266	299425.6	298862	563.59
14-Jun-18	1,122.04			266	298462.6	298862	-399.3
15-Jun-18	1,124.94	4	4499.76	270	303733.8	303361.7	372.07
18-Jun-18	1,123.99			270	303477.3	303361.7	115.57
19-Jun-18	1,114.81			270	300998.7	303361.7	-2363
20-Jun-18	1,119.65			270	302305.5	303361.7	-1056
21-Jun-18	1,115.29			270	301128.3	303361.7	-2233
22-Jun-18	1,124.79	4	4499.16	274	308192.5	307860.9	331.57
25-Jun-18	1,118.35			274	306427.9	307860.9	-1433
26-Jun-18	1,121.32			274	307241.7	307860.9	-619.2
27-Jun-18	1,107.76			274	303526.2	307860.9	-4335
28-Jun-18	1,100.53			274	301545.2	307860.9	-6316
29-Jun-18	1,111.88	4	4447.52	278	309102.6	312308.4	-3206
02-Jul-18	1,109.97			278	308571.7	312308.4	-3737

Date	Close	Buy Share	Investment	Total Share	Market Value at Close	Basic Investment Value	Profit/ Loss
03-Jul-18	1,114.04			278	309703.1	312308.4	-2605
04-Jul-18	1,118.75			278	311012.5	312308.4	-1296
05-Jul-18	1,119.13			278	311118.1	312308.4	-1190
06-Jul-18	1,123.02	4	4492.08	282	316691.6	316800.5	-108.8
09-Jul-18	1,128.54			282	318248.3	316800.5	1447.8
Next Day Sell Quantity					1		
Estimated Profit Taking					1128.54		
10-Jul-18	1,137.27			281	319572.9	316800.5	2772.4
Next Day Sell Quantity					2		
Estimated Profit Taking					2274.54		
11-Jul-18	1,137.26			279	317295.5	316800.5	495.05
12-Jul-18	1,144.95			279	319441.1	316800.5	2640.6
13-Jul-18	1,146.32	4	4585.28	283	324408.6	321385.8	3022.8
Next Day Sell Quantity					3		
Estimated Profit Taking					3438.96		
16-Jul-18	1,139.83			280	319152.4	321385.8	-2233
17-Jul-18	1,144.85			280	320558	321385.8	-827.8

Date	Close	Buy Share	Investment	Total Share	Market Value at Close	Basic Investment Value	Profit/ Loss
18-Jul-18	1,141.18			280	319530.4	321385.8	-1855
19-Jul-18	1,141.21			280	319538.8	321385.8	-1847
20-Jul-18	1,149.30	4	4597.2	284	326401.2	325983	418.23
23-Jul-18	1,153.40			284	327565.6	325983	1582.6
Next Day Sell Quantity						1	
Estimated Profit Taking						1153.40	
24-Jul-18	1,157.12			283	327465	325983	1482
Next Day Sell Quantity						1	
Estimated Profit Taking						1157.12	
25-Jul-18	1,159.19			282	326891.6	325983	908.61
26-Jul-18	1,161.58			282	327565.6	325983	1582.6
27-Jul-18	1,173.23	4	4692.92	286	335543.8	330675.9	4867.9
Next Day Sell Quantity						4	
Estimated Profit Taking						4692.92	
30-Jul-18	1,177.42			282	332032.4	330675.9	1356.6
Next Day Sell Quantity						1	

Date	Close	Buy Share	Investment	Total Share	Market Value at Close	Basic Investment Value	Profit/ Loss
Estimated Profit Taking					1177.42		
31-Jul-18	1,182.50			281	332282.5	330675.9	1606.6
Next Day Sell Quantity					1		
Estimated Profit Taking					1182.50		
01-Aug-18	1,181.24			280	330747.2	330675.9	71.31
02-Aug-18	1,174.29			280	328801.2	330675.9	-1875
03-Aug-18	1,186.19	4	4744.76	284	336878	335420.7	1457.3
Next Day Sell Quantity					1		
Estimated Profit Taking					1186.19		
06-Aug-18	1,187.35			283	336020.1	335420.7	599.4
07-Aug-18	1,187.39			283	336031.4	335420.7	610.72
08-Aug-18	1,191.71			283	337253.9	335420.7	1833.3
Next Day Sell Quantity					1		
Estimated Profit Taking					1191.71		
09-Aug-18	1,193.11			282	336457	335420.7	1036.4
Next Day Sell Quantity					1		
Estimated Profit taking					1193.11		

Thus, during these 15 months, we increased our basic investment to Rs. 3,35,420.70 by buying NIFTY BeES for Rs. 5000 every week and as and when profit exceeded Rs. 1000, we sold as many shares as required just to take our profit out. This way, our tree has enabled us to book profits amounting to Rs. 40,385.48 during these 15 months; this was around 12% of the basic investment. These profits were also almost income tax-free as the profits on whatever few units we sold after one year were entirely tax-free.

Now, let's discuss a concern that may potentially arise in your mind. Possibly, there may be some of my readers who may get shocked to see the current market price of NIFTY BeES fluctuating around Rs. 100 and may wonder how its price crashed from Rs. 1193 straight down to Rs. 100.

The fact is that NIFTY BeES had split its face value. Earlier, its value used to be 1/10th of NIFTY; it has since been revised to 1/100th of NIFTY. That means, people already holding shares were allotted 10 new shares to replace one old share. For instance, a holding of old 282 shares converted to a holding of 2820 shares and accordingly, the price of one share also came down to 1/10th of previous price. In other words, the current price of Rs. 100 is actually equivalent to Rs. 1000 of that period.

If you still find the importance of profit booking during those 15 months, as per data above, insignificant, you should remember that the price of NIFTY BeES had gone up to Rs. 142.95 during March 2020. Just imagine the amount of profit we could have booked by that time. Similarly, during market slump, its price had gone down to Rs. 81 on 23 March, 2020. This later recovered and the price of a unit of NIFTY BeES was around Rs. 100 in May 2020. That means, had you kept your system active till date, not only your holding of units would have kept growing but also, in any market condition, your profit booking would have continued, that also entirely tax-free, as you would have had enough units older than 1 year to sell with long term capital gains.

Continuing with the above process, your holding would have grown to 7500 shares and after that, a one rupee increase in NIFTY BeES would have enabled you to book a profit of Rs. 7500. Hence, you would have then written covered calls. Even if the market had gone up after that and NIFTY BeES price had increased by Rs. 10, the system would have automatically booked the profit of Rs. 75000, and in case you had to pay any amount towards your covered call, you could have paid out of that profit of Rs. 75000. Thus, in this method, it's not necessary to accumulate 9500 units before writing covered calls. Once an automatic system is established, you may write one covered call even after accumulating 7500 units; that call has to be sold for strike price 5% above spot price.

Hence, the real fun comes only when you, following the above method, first accumulate 7500 units of NIFTY ETF and then keep the system active for automatic profit booking with every market upturn.

Let's take an example. NIFTY is at 10116 on 10 June, 2020. You have to write call of 5% above the same. Adding 5% profit to 10116 makes it 10621.80. Hence, you have to write a call of 10600 for expiry of 25 June, 2020. You would receive premium at the rate of Rs. 61, totalling to Rs. 4575. The margin required for writing the call may be obtained by pledging your holding of 7500 units of NIFTY BeES.

If NIFTY closes above 10600 on 25 June, 2020, you may have to pay some amount. If NIFTY stays at 10600, the entire premium of Rs. 4575 is all yours as rent for enjoying the shade of your tree. Whether NIFTY remains static or goes down, this rent of Rs. 4575 is all yours.

If NIFTY closes at 11000 on expiry, you would have to pay Rs. 30000 towards your call of 10600. However, in this case, the price of unit in your holding would also go up at least by Rs. 10, thus making a profit of Rs. 75000 on your holding of 7500 units. Even if you pay Rs. 30000 out of the same, what difference it makes to you?

Moreover, NIFTY is not going to rise by 5% every month. Most of the time, you would get the rent for allowing somebody to sit under the shade of your tree, without doing anything. Many a times, NIFTY may keep rising for some time and fall around expiry. This would allow your system to keep booking profits and when NIFTY crashes at expiry, the entire premium also would be yours.

You should definitely grow this tree in your house. You may plant a Bank NIFTY tree also. Instead of indulging in useless trades, keep enjoying the fruits of these trees. Once your have accumulated 7500 units, you not only enjoy the fruits but also earn rent for its shade by way of premium on calls written for strike price 5% above spot price. When your holding grows over 15000 units, you may write 2 calls and when the holding goes beyond 22500, you may write 3 calls, and by the time you reach this level, you would have earned enough to consider your entire holding to be just free of cost.

This is what is called financial freedom. If you have enough funds, or if your are not able to control yourself, you may straightaway buy 7500 units, initiate an SIP of Rs. 5000 and start charging rent for sitting under the shade of your tree from today itself.

A person spends Rs. 40 lacs to build a house. If he rents the same out, he gets hardly Rs. 10000 per month. Here, if we have NIFTY ETF for Rs. 40 lacs, we may write 5 covered calls and earn around Rs. 20000 towards premium even when

NIFTY does not go up. And if NIFTY does go up, your holding of Rs. 40 lacs would make enough profit to provide for payments towards your covered calls.

You should also remember that we may even plant trees for top 5 or 10 different NIFTY-based ETFs having maximum volumes instead of investing your entire capital in NIFTY ETF only.

A doubt and its resolution: The digital e-book edition of this book was made available on Amazon and Google Play Store on 24 June, 2020. After reading that book, one of my followers requested through email to resolve one of his doubts. I found his doubt entirely reasonable and felt that other readers also may have the same doubt in their minds. Hence, I thought it proper to include that doubt and its resolution in this print edition.

Here is the query from this follower by name Sachin Kalebagh. "I have gone through your book '*Option Trading Se Paison Ka Ped Kaise Lagayen*?' I have also read Chapter 10 of the same titled '*Paison Ka Ped Kaise Lagayen Jiske Phal Mile Bagair Income Tax Chukaye*'. You have mentioned that profits exceeding Rs. 1000 should be taken out by selling ETF shares next day. Accordingly, you have shown in the table that after getting a profit of 1245.70, the same has been booked by selling one share for Rs. 1008.18.

"But you have booked real profit of Rs. 32.92 only. If you adjust STT, brokerage etc., you have made a profit of Rs. 13 only. This Rs. 13 only and not Rs. 1008.18, is your actual profit (1008.18 is actually the sale price of your one share; how did you take that as your profit?). That means, you have earned a net profit of Rs. 13 on your basic investment of Rs. 975.26; that is just 1.3% profit.

"Computing on the same lines, during the entire 15 months, you sold shares for Rs. 40385.48 against your basic investment of Rs. 335420.70. But this Rs. 40385.48 is not your real profit. Your real profit is Rs. 4400 only after adjusting the original cost (Rs. 36000 approximately) of those shares. And as profit of Rs. 4400 is made on the basic investment of Rs. 335420.70, you made an overall profit of only 1.3% again. Don't you find this 1.3% profit in 15 months too low?"

I responded to the follower with the answer as below:

This is the beauty of this method. If you look at it from the point of view of Income Tax regulations, we booked a profit of Rs. 13 only and hence paid negligible or zero income tax. But, **in fact, we did not reduce even a rupee from our basic investment in the sheet. According to you, as we made a profit of Rs. 13 by selling one share, we should have reduced the relevant original investment also.** But, we did not reduce the basic investment value for subsequent computations. In other words, we are not focusing on the value at which we are buying or selling the shares; rather our main focus is on the tree. There are thus two points—first is our basic investment and the second is the profit being made on that investment.

For instance, suppose basic investment is 100 and its value at market price is 110. If we take 10 rupees out of that 110, the original investment of 100 is still intact. It's a different question how we take that Rs. 10 out, but the investment amount is not altered. Hence, in scientific and mathematical terms, isn't this amount of 10 rupees a profit?

In fact, this method is based on amazing science. Out of the profit of Rs. 1008 that we booked without altering the basic investment amount, Rs. 13 has been booked from current profit and the rest 1008 – 13 = 995 rupees has been booked in advance against the profits to be generated in future, and hence the basic investment has not been reduced.

Hope you would have got the point that if we do not reduce the basic investment, the increase in value of the same would be our profit and though selling units to realise that profit would reduce the number of units in our holding but the average value of the remaining units or shares would go up in the same proportion such that they would come in profit in future only after recovering the profits booked earlier.

Thus, this money tree is really amazing. It just has two deficiencies. Firstly, this requires you to keep computing the basic investment and profit on an Excel sheet separately. You may not probably like to invest the effort of 5 minutes on a daily basis towards the same.

Secondly, being a fully automatic system, this may not provide you cricket-like excitement that you get in looking for the tips for the shares having potential to make you rich overnight and then buying and holding the same. But this tree is very useful for covered calls and ratio spread method. You may probably experience the same excitement that you got earlier by trading on daily basis, following the method discussed in the next chapter.

□

11

Ratio Spread Method and Its Usage

Gradually, as time passed by, Ghisu Bhai started working first with the 4-stroke method in NIFTY and Bank NIFTY, as suggested by me. He invested all the profits he made out of the same in a money tree using NIFTY ETF following the method explained in the previous chapter, in order to avail the benefits of covered calls.

After some time, Ghisu Bhai had enough units to take up covered call writing. His money tree was also growing constantly and bearing fruits for him. Now, he had started to earn from weekly premiums on covered calls also and he was getting into a mood to take some risk.

Ghisu Bhai said, "Please tell me some method for options where, though little risk may be involved, the chances of reward in proportion to the risk are more".

Hence, considering the risk-taking capacity of Ghisu Bhai and availability of adequate margin with him, I started to explain the Ratio Spread Method to him. The Ratio Spread method involves buying and selling of calls/puts in the ratio of 1:2. There is a reverse method also where calls and puts are bought and sold in the ratio of 2:1. This is called Backspread.

Ghisu Bhai was finding it a bit difficult to grasp the points. However, he was now familiar with my style and he knew that I would explain every point with examples. He was hence keeping calm.

There are four types of Ratio Spread:

1. Call Ratio Spread
2. Put Ratio Spread
3. Call ratio Backspread
4. Put ratio Backspread

(1) Call ratio Spread: In this, we have to buy 1 In the Money call and then sell (write) 2 Out of the Money calls of higher strike prices such that the total of the premiums received on writing these 2 calls exceeds the premium paid for buying the above 1 call. To understand this practically, I opened the screen on 26 May, 2020 for NIFTY options expiring on 25 June, 2020 for Ghisu Bhai to have a look. The screen looked like the one below.

NIFTY was trading at 9105.30 at that time. If you look at the above screen carefully, you may find In the Money call of 9100 being quoted the 'Ask Price' of 273.60. That means, if you buy 1 In the Money call of 9100, you would have to pay 75 × 273.60 = 20,520 rupees as premium. On the other hand, please have a look at the 'Bid Price' of Out of the Money call of 9400; somebody is interested to buy the same even at a premium of 147.45. Thus, if you sell 2 calls of 9400, you would get 147.45 × 2 × 75 = 22117.50 rupees as premium. In other words, you are able to buy 1 call of 9100 spending 20520 towards premium by using funds out of 22117.50 received as premium for 2 calls sold. You saved an amount of 22117.50 – 20520 = 1597.50 rupees in this deal. Holding the deals till expiry on 25 June, 2020 would have resulted profits and losses depending

CALLS												PUTS		
IV	LTP	CHNG	BID QTY	BID PRICE	ASK PRICE	ASK QTY	STRIKE PRICE	BID QTY	BID PRICE	ASK PRICE	ASK QTY	CHNG	LTP	IV
-	875.00	46.15	75	824.95	840.50	75	8,300.00	75	78.00	78.70	75	-26.20	77.90	35.37
-	-	-	7,350	631.40	931.65	7,350	8,350.00	150	11.60	112.60	150	-	-	-
-	771.80	26.00	75	747.75	756.25	75	8,400.00	75	94.95	95.40	75	-28.55	95.10	34.92
-	-	-	7,350	589.65	846.75	7,350	8,450.00	150	52.10	130.70	150	-	-	-
20.91	672.90	3.30	150	668.60	672.15	75	8,500.00	225	114.15	114.55	150	-30.00	114.35	34.30
-	-	-	7,350	488.80	724.60	7,350	8,550.00	150	115.90	125.00	75	-1,321.70	120.00	-
23.09	612.00	24.95	75	589.35	597.90	300	8,600.00	75	135.80	136.35	75	-29.85	136.70	33.48
-	-	-	4,950	549.05	575.65	4,950	8,650.00	75	140.75	153.00	150	-1,356.10	142.05	-
23.01	536.00	2.95	75	515.50	523.50	75	8,700.00	150	163.15	163.70	75	-35.50	162.65	33.07
-	-	-	4,950	481.75	507.85	4,950	8,750.00	150	155.05	187.45	150	-	-	-
23.45	464.80	10.35	150	450.05	452.95	75	8,800.00	225	192.40	192.80	75	-34.00	192.70	32.64
-	-	-	4,950	413.25	439.55	4,950	8,850.00	75	106.05	242.00	75	-	-	-
23.69	385.65	-4.95	150	385.90	387.50	75	8,900.00	75	226.05	227.05	75	-36.20	226.60	32.26
24.74	406.90	57.30	4,950	348.35	374.40	75	8,950.00	75	234.80	249.30	225	-47.10	230.00	32.66
23.96	326.60	-5.10	150	327.25	328.55	75	9,000.00	75	265.75	266.30	150	-38.50	267.30	31.89
23.87	310.00	-2.25	75	300.15	305.35	75	9,050.00	1,125	281.05	286.95	1,125	-50.80	270.00	32.03
23.89	272.60	-5.00	150	272.60	273.60	150	9,100.00	75	310.60	311.60	75	-47.90	310.00	31.57
24.19	259.00	2.85	1,125	248.55	253.95	1,125	9,150.00	1,125	328.55	334.45	1,125	-1,484.75	310.00	-

CALLS													PUTS	
IV	LTP	CHNG	BID QTY	BID PRICE	ASK PRICE	ASK QTY	STRIKE PRICE	BID QTY	BID PRICE	ASK PRICE	ASK QTY	CHNG	LTP	IV
23.94	225.00	-9.35	75	225.70	226.50	150	9,200.00	225	361.50	363.25	75	-45.20	361.65	31.79
-	-	-	150	201.20	212.40	600	9,250.00	4,950	375.65	401.35	4,950	-	-	-
24.02	184.30	-4.80	75	183.45	183.95	150	9,300.00	75	418.95	420.65	75	-44.30	418.30	31.51
-	-	-	75	158.75	177.85	4,950	9,350.00	75	432.15	456.05	4,950	-	-	-
23.89	147.35	-5.65	75	147.45	147.90	75	9,400.00	150	482.40	484.95	150	-41.05	484.95	31.62
23.50	141.00	-41.00	300	1.50	-	-	9,450.00	4,950	500.55	524.05	4,950	-	-	-
23.90	117.20	-7.35	75	117.10	117.45	75	9,500.00	75	552.95	556.15	75	-39.65	553.10	32.19
-	-	-	3,000	3.60	180.45	7,350	9,550.00	4,950	571.45	597.70	4,950	-	-	-
23.82	90.60	-6.85	225	91.05	91.40	75	9,600.00	75	624.75	633.85	75	-61.15	618.00	33.02
-	-	-	75	9.00	158.25	7,350	9,650.00	7,350	471.00	731.90	7,350	-	-	-
23.63	70.00	-7.10	75	70.05	70.30	75	9,700.00	375	702.35	711.55	75	-49.30	702.70	33.97
-	-	-	7,500	30.00	140.50	7,350	9,750.00	7,350	517.90	816.90	7,350	-	-	-
23.60	53.35	-7.30	75	53.45	53.90	75	9,800.00	150	786.65	795.50	75	-38.70	786.25	36.02
-	-	-	7,500	23.25	124.40	7,350	9,850.00	7,350	596.50	908.05	7,350	-	-	-

on the conditions as below:

1. Had the market fallen below 9100, to any extent, you would have been still left with Rs. 1597.50 towards difference in premiums as your profit. In other words, close price of 9100, 9000, 8950, 8900, 8700, 7500, 5000 or even 0 on expiry would have allowed you to retain that difference of Rs. 1597.50 in premiums as profit.
2. Had NIFTY closed at 9150 on expiry, you would have earned a profit of Rs. 50 on your call of 9100 i.e. you would have received 50 × 75 = 3750 rupees. Additionally, Rs. 1597.50 towards difference in premiums also would have been saved, thus giving you a total gain of Rs. 5347.50.
3. Had NIFTY closed at 9200 on expiry, you would have made a profit of Rs. 100 on your call of 9100, thus earning Rs. 7500 for the lot. Along with Rs. 1597.50 towards difference in premiums, your total profit would have been Rs. 9097.50.
4. NIFTY expiring at 9250 would have given you Rs. 12847.50.
5. Had NIFTY expired at 9300, you would have earned Rs. 15000 on your call of 9100, making your total profit to Rs. 16,597.50 after adding Rs. 1597.50 towards difference in premiums.
6. NIFTY expiring at 9350 would have resulted in a profit of 18750 + 1597.50 = 20347.50 rupees.
7. NIFTY expiring at 9400 would have resulted in a profit of 22500 + 1597.50 = 24097.50 rupees.
8. Had NIFTY closed at 9450 on expiry, you would have received an amount of 350 × 75 = 26250 rupees on your call of 9100. However, on account of loss of

Rs. 50 on 2 calls of 9400 written by you, you would have had to pay 75 × 2 × 50 = 7500 rupees. Thus, you would have been left with Rs. 18750 only. That along with the amount of Rs. 1597.50 towards difference in premiums would have still made your total profit to Rs. 20347.50.

9. NIFTY closed at 9500 on expiry.

   Initial credit = 1597.50
   Profit on call of 9100 = 30,000.00
   Total receipt = 31,597.50

   And, you would have had to pay Rs. 15000 on 2 calls of 9400. Thus, your total profit would have been 31597.50 – 15000 = 16,597.50 rupees.
10. Now, without going into more of calculations, I am telling you straightaway that you would have made a profit of Rs. 12847.50 if NIFTY had expired at 9550.
11. Had NIFTY expired at 9600, you would have made a profit of Rs. 9172.50.
12. Let me go into detailed calculation again. Had NIFTY closed at 9650 on expiry, you would have received on your call of 9100 an amount of 550 × 75 = 41250 rupees but, on account of loss of 250 × 2 = 500 points on your 2 calls sold, you would have had to pay 500 × 75 = 37500 rupees. You would have still be left with Rs. 3750 and that along with initial credit of Rs. 1597.50 would have made your total profit to Rs. 5347.50.

Have a look at the positions after that.

Sl. No.	Level of Expiry	Profit / Loss
1	9700	1597.50 Profit
2	9750	– 2152.50 Loss
3	9800	– 5902.50 Loss
4	9850	– 9652.50 Loss
5	9900	– 13402.50 Loss
6	9950	– 17152.50 Loss
7	10,000	– 20902.50 Loss

But, in reality, nobody waits for that level of expiry, and it's not advisable also to do so. But, why should you not wait? You will find answer to the same in the last chapter 'Conclusion' of this book.

If you want, you may exit in intraday itself in this Call Ratio Spread method after booking profit/loss. The possibility of NIFTY jumping straight from 9105.30 to a level above 9700 on the same day was almost nil. NIFTY had actually closed at 9029.50 on 26 May, 2020. You had already bought 1 In the Money call of 9100. Then, had you decided to exit intraday by booking loss/profit, you would have incurred loss on your call of 9100. But, your 2 calls of 9400 that you had sold received the benefit of Theta of time, as their market price also went down. For your benefit, I have taken the screen shot (below) of the position after close of market on 26 May, 2020.

The last trading price of the call of 9100 at the close of market was 252.95, Thus, had you sold call of 9100 that you had bought at 273.60 in intraday at 252.95 just before the close of market, you would have incurred a loss for the lot of 75 at the rate of 20.65, totalling to Rs. 1548.75.

Similarly, you had sold (shorted) 2 calls of 9400 at 147.45; last trading price of that call in intraday was 135. Hence, you could have squared off your position by buying two calls of

CALLS													PUTS	
IV	LTP	CHNG	BID QTY	BID PRICE	ASK PRICE	ASK QTY	STRIKE PRICE	BID QTY	BID PRICE	ASK PRICE	ASK QTY	CHNG	LTP	IV
-	792.00	-36.85	75	802.50	823.20	75	8,300.00	150	76.50	77.80	75	-26.80	77.30	35.37
-	-	-	7,350	575.45	870.30	7,350	8,350.00	150	26.25	115.30	150	-	-	-
-	734.00	-11.80	75	728.10	734.00	75	8,400.00	75	92.05	92.90	75	-30.95	92.70	34.92
-	-	-	7,350	514.15	778.00	7,350	8,450.00	150	8.25	117.55	75	-1,275.20	111.00	-
20.91	652.85	-16.75	75	651.00	654.35	75	8,500.00	75	111.75	113.40	75	-32.35	112.00	34.30
-	-	-	7,350	384.75	667.60	7,350	8,550.00	75	118.95	124.95	75	-1,317.75	123.95	-
23.09	570.00	-17.05	75	566.40	582.05	75	8,600.00	75	133.10	137.55	75	-33.00	133.55	33.48
-	-	-	-	-	607.50	7,350	8,650.00	75	140.30	160.40	375	-1,350.65	147.50	-
23.01	499.95	-33.10	750	497.55	508.45	75	8,700.00	75	159.05	165.10	75	-38.15	160.00	33.07
-	-	-	7,500	0.05	517.20	7,350	8,750.00	150	166.55	192.35	75	-1,356.60	199.00	-
23.45	432.95	-21.50	750	432.05	433.00	150	8,800.00	75	190.50	191.00	75	-34.70	192.00	32.64
-	-	-	-	-	481.25	7,350	8,850.00	75	103.70	247.40	150	-	-	-
23.69	370.00	-20.60	675	363.10	369.90	75	8,900.00	75	225.05	226.00	600	-37.70	225.10	32.26
24.74	328.20	-21.40	-	-	399.10	7,350	8,950.00	150	164.45	255.95	75	-31.10	246.00	32.66
23.96	308.00	-23.70	150	308.00	309.00	150	9,000.00	1,500	264.10	266.70	900	-39.80	266.00	31.89
23.87	281.00	-31.25	75	278.10	281.00	750	9,050.00	75	280.00	291.70	75	-36.60	284.20	32.03
23.89	252.95	-24.65	750	252.95	256.00	150	9,100.00	75	310.10	313.00	75	-46.40	311.50	31.57
24.19	223.10	-33.05	150	158.50	264.95	150	9,150.00	-	-	-	-	-1,530.45	264.30	-

CALLS													PUTS	
IV	LTP	CHNG	BID QTY	BID PRICE	ASK PRICE	ASK QTY	STRIKE PRICE	BID QTY	BID PRICE	ASK PRICE	ASK QTY	CHNG	LTP	IV
24.19	223.10	-33.05	150	158.50	264.95	150	9,150.00	-	-	-	-	-1,530.45	264.30	-
23.94	209.70	-24.65	750	207.05	209.70	600	9,200.00	75	361.45	363.00	75	-43.90	362.95	31.79
-	-	-	150	1.05	-	-	9,250.00	75	332.15	463.45	7,350	-	-	-
24.02	167.95	-21.15	750	166.05	168.00	75	9,300.00	75	422.10	428.95	75	-40.50	422.10	31.51
-	-	-	75	7.35	-	-	9,350.00	75	325.60	539.60	7,350	-	-	-
23.89	135.00	-18.00	75	132.00	136.40	75	9,400.00	75	484.60	498.75	75	-36.05	489.95	31.62
23.50	130.00	-52.00	75	108.80	-	-	9,450.00	300	370.90	609.35	7,350	-1,414.05	569.45	-
23.90	104.90	-19.65	150	103.00	104.70	75	9,500.00	900	555.65	564.20	75	-30.40	562.35	32.19
-	87.00	-1,199.5	3,000	3.60	146.75	150	9,550.00	75	468.90	673.95	75	-	-	-

9400 at the rate of 135. In this deal, you would have made a profit at the rate of 147.45 – 135 = 12.45 for each call, totalling to Rs. 1867.50 for two lots of 75 each. This way, you could have exited in intraday itself by making a net profit of 1867.50 – 1548.75 = 318.75 rupees.

By the same logic, you may book your profit/loss by exiting your position any time before expiry. Just think, had the market gone up (actually it did) from 9105.30 to 9200 within 5 to 7 days, it would have been natural for the premium on your call of 9100 to go up and, due to loss of time (Theta), the premium on the call of 9400 to go down. In the circumstances, closing your positions would have given you a profit somewhere between Rs. 4000 and Rs. 5000 within a period of 5-7 days only.

In Call Ratio Spread method, profit in an uptrend is limited whereas the same is secured in downtrend. Hence, if the market keeps falling or is not going up significantly, you should estimate your profit/loss on daily basis under this strategy, and book your profits the moment you see a gain of over Rs. 2000.

In an unpredictable market, you should exit your positions with whatever insignificant loss of around 1000 to 1500 it results into, the moment you find the market bouncing up by 500 points.

The best strategy in intraday market is to take position at the very opening of the market and exit just before close of the market with whatever profit you are making on account of Theta. In this strategy, the loss, if any, incurred in intraday would be minimal while you would have more chances of gains only.

Also, if you have already planted your money tree as

suggested in the previous chapter, you may, instead of selling covered calls, use this Call Ratio Spread method. You would enjoy the same. You may pledge your NIFTY ETF for margin and then forget after creating this call ratio spread. Howsoever big jump NIFTY makes on expiry, your loss would be less in comparison to direct covered calls. Also, increase in price of NIFTY ETF and hence the value of your holding would make your tree bear lots of fruits that would comfortably cover any payments that you may have to make because of increase in price.

Share Genius Method for Call Ratio Spread

Ghisu Bhai asked, "Can we use this method to earn money by buying Out of the Money calls also?"

I told him that the same was possible. The market does provide such opportunities many times. Let me explain to you one more Share Genius method of limited Call Ratio Spread.

In this, you have to buy 1 Out of the Money call and short 2 Out of the Money calls in intraday in a way that you are still left with some credit with all positions put together. Going back to the examples above, when NIFTY was at 9105.30 on 26 May, 2020, the Out of the Money call of 9500 with expiry of 25 June, 2020 was available at 117.45 and the premium on the call of 9700 was 70.05. Thus, had we bought one call of 9500 at 117.45 and sold 2 calls of 9700 at 70.05, we would have received 70.05 × 2 = 140.10 rupees as premium and paid a premium of 117.45, thus retaining a credit of 22.65 points. That means, had NIFTY remained below 9500 till expiry, we would have made a profit of 1698.75. Instead, had we closed our positions in intraday itself, we would have sold our call of 9500 at 104.90 incurring a loss of 117.45 – 104.90 = 12.55 and bought 2 calls of 9700 at 60.95 earning a profit of 70.05 – 60.95

= 9.10 × 2 = 18.20, i.e. a net gain of 18.20 – 12.55 = 5.65 points. Thus, we would have made a profit of 423.75 in intraday itself. In this method, we would have made profit even if NIFTY had gone up to a level of 10,500. Hence, if you hold this spread for some days and keep a close eye on the positions, you may make a reasonably good profit.

Put Ratio Spread: In this method, 1 In the Money put is bought and 2 Out of the Money puts are sold in such a way that the sum of premiums received on 2 puts sold is more than the premium paid on 1 put bought. In other words, we have to write 2 such puts that earn us premium that is at least 20 to 40 points more than the premium paid for buying 1 In the Money put. Here, the figure of 20-40 points is not a fixed value and you may, if you so wish, keep it more or less, but overall, you should be left with some profit on premiums. To explain this practically, let me show you the NIFTY option chain as at 1 PM on 27 May, 2020 for expiry on 25 June, 2020. NIFTY was at 9,153.30 at that time and the put of 9,200 was In the Money put.

For buying put, the Ask Price for put of 9200 was 307.20. Thus, 1 put of 9200 would cost a total premium of 307.20 × 75 = 23040 rupees. We can see that the Bid Price for put of 8900 was 185.95, i.e. somebody was ready to buy 2 lots of put of 8900 at 185.95.

If we sell (write or short) 2 lots of put of 8900, we would get 185.95 × 2 = 371.90 as premium. Thus, we spent 307.20 to buy a put and received 371.90 after selling 2 puts and overall, got a fantastic credit of 64.70 points in this deal. I am calling this 'fantastic' because, if you don't do anything till expiry and NIFTY closes above 9200 on expiry on 25 June, 2020, you would get 64.70 × 75 = 4852.50 rupees against that credit of 64.70.

CALLS									PUTS							
Volume	IV	LTP	Net Chng	Bid Qty	Bid Price	Ask Price	Ask Qty	Strike Price	Bid Qty	Bid Price	Ask Price	Ask Qty	Net Chng	LTP	IV	Volume
38	25.23	626.65	63.65	375	640.35	648.85	375	8600.00	75	108.30	108.55	75	-29.05	108.55	33.03	3,147
-	-	-	-	4,950	587.90	613.30	4,950	8650.00	75	115.45	121.35	75	-32.25	118.50	33.01	363
105	21.96	565.00	74.40	75	563.80	568.85	75	8700.00	225	129.80	130.20	75	-35.45	129.60	32.68	4,444
-	-	-	-	4,950	512.10	537.50	4,950	8750.00	75	137.90	145.45	75	-56.15	142.85	-	9
414	22.60	492.35	68.55	75	491.35	494.30	75	8800.00	225	156.10	156.65	75	-40.75	156.40	32.52	6,940
-	-	-	-	4,950	443.95	469.40	4,950	8850.00	4,950	163.20	178.60	75	-	-	-	-
549	23.34	424.55	62.85	150	421.55	423.85	1,125	8900.00	150	185.95	186.15	525	-46.10	186.00	31.93	2,924
-	-	-	-	4,950	374.30	399.25	4,950	8950.00	75	200.20	204.50	75	-44.60	206.00	32.59	32
9,098	22.64	358.00	57.90	75	357.00	357.70	75	9000.00	300	220.50	221.35	75	-52.60	220.50	31.71	13,108
288	22.71	323.90	50.20	75	325.30	327.40	75	9050.00	75	239.05	240.00	75	-49.65	242.00	30.86	168
4,398	22.74	298.00	50.15	75	297.00	297.85	75	9100.00	75	259.90	260.80	75	-59.70	260.00	31.77	3,145
76	24.01	272.50	45.05	75	269.25	273.75	75	9150.00	1,125	281.10	285.05	75	20.75	285.05	-	12
6,070	22.83	244.95	42.60	150	244.35	245.00	75	9200.00	75	305.90	307.20	150	-64.50	306.75	31.57	1,897
-	-	-	-	75	216.20	227.45	600	9250.00	4,950	321.35	345.05	150	-	-	-	-
4,876	22.71	199.10	37.00	75	198.85	199.40	150	9300.00	150	360.00	361.00	75	-72.50	359.90	31.33	271
-	-	-	-	150	165.70	184.90	4,950	9350.00	4,950	376.25	400.95	75	-	-	-	-
4,599	22.81	159.20	30.60	75	158.05	158.75	150	9400.00	300	419.00	421.60	150	-76.85	420.00	32.90	280
1	-	93.20	-36.80	75	101.00	-	-	9450.00	4,950	443.75	464.45	4,950	-36.35	533.10	30.97	1
14,787	22.98	125.25	24.25	75	125.45	125.85	150	9500.00	75	487.55	488.50	75	-81.90	488.55	33.30	2,946
11	-	104.00	17.00	75	106.30	111.30	75	9550.00	75	511.30	536.20	75	-	-	-	-
4,098	23.01	96.40	17.45	75	96.15	96.50	225	9600.00	450	551.50	558.50	150	-86.05	555.00	34.15	83

CALLS									PUTS							
Volume	IV	LTP	Net Chng	Bid Qty	Bid Price	Ask Price	Ask Qty	Strike Price	Bid Qty	Bid Price	Ask Price	Ask Qty	Net Chng	LTP	IV	Volume
4,422	23.05	72.70	12.85	600	72.60	72.75	75	9700.00	150	624.80	634.70	75	-66.20	648.00	-	6
-	-	-	-	1,200	25.20	88.75	150	9750.00	75	578.45	739.70	75	-	-	-	-
5,097	23.34	53.65	7.45	75	53.45	53.80	225	9800.00	150	706.90	715.15	225	-99.70	716.00	36.68	22
-	-	-	-	1,200	16.20	88.85	150	9850.00	75	711.20	862.75	75	-	-	-	-
2,847	23.60	40.05	4.35	75	39.90	40.10	75	9900.00	150	793.20	801.05	150	-104.85	805.00	31.37	19
-	-	-	-	1,200	14.20	78.35	150	9950.00	525	760.25	923.40	7,425	-	-	-	-
9,782	23.95	29.95	3.05	75	29.85	30.00	4,350	10000.00	150	883.00	888.80	75	-108.30	886.00	39.08	832
-	-	-	-	1,200	9.60	68.40	300	10050.00	7,350	851.20	1,063.65	7,350	-	-	-	-
710	24.00	20.85	0.70	75	20.70	21.20	75	10100.00	225	969.00	980.65	75	-66.25	1,014.95	-	23

The chart below shows what you would get if NIFTY expires below 9200.

Sl. No.	Level on Expiry on 25 June	Profit/Loss on Put of 9200	Profit/Loss on 2 Puts shorted	Net Profit/ Loss
1	9200 and above	–	4852.50	4852.50
2	9150	3750	4852.50	8602.50
3	9100	7500	4852.50	12352.50
4	9050	11250	4852.50	16102.50
5	9000	15000	4852.50	19852.50
6	8950	18750	4852.50	23602.50
7	8900	22500	4852.50	27352.50
8	8850	26250	–2647.50	23602.50
9	8800	30000	–10147.50	19852.50
10	8750	33750	–17647.50	16102.50
11	8700	37500	–25147.50	12352.50
12	8650	41250	–32647.50	8602.50
13	8600	45000	–40147.50	4852.50
14	8550	48750	–47647.50	1102.50
15	8500	52500	–55147.50	–2647.50
16	8450	56250	–62647.50	–6397.50

Thus, you may see, you would have incurred loss in this strategy only if NIFTY had closed below 8550 on expiry. As I have said earlier, you may book profit even in intraday under this strategy, and you may also book profit anytime later without waiting for the expiry.

Your loss starts only when NIFTY starts going below 8550. Just think how safe you are in this method. We are making profit even up to the fall of 6% in NIFTY and in the case of NIFTY going up, we would be in profit at any level of jump. Ghisu Bhai asked, "If this method is so safe, why most of the people don't use it?"

I replied, "It again comes back to the same point that option market has been structured in a way that it is advantageous for traders having large capitals and disadvantageous for small investors. In this method, a large amount of margin, say around 3 to 4 lacs of rupees, is required for writing 2 puts, and small investors do not hedge the same by buying 1 put. Margin is again required for buying a put. Small investors normally do not have that much of margin amount. However, if somebody follows my suggestion and plants a money tree i.e. buys units of NIFTY ETF and gradually accumulates units worth Rs. 10 lacs, he may get an amount of Rs. 8 lacs, assuming 20% haircut, for margin money by pledging that holding. **In the case of a deal in futures, MTM margin is settled in cash. In other words, if at the end of the day, your deal in futures needs additional margin, you cannot pay the same using collateral margin against pledged ETFs/stocks; you need cash for the same. However, there is no such condition in the case of an option deal. Collateral margin (margin availed against pledged stocks/ETFs) may be used for options till expiry. Hence, most of the traders consider it better to take positions in options instead of futures.**

Now, let's see the position of the put ratio spread created by us on 27 May, 2020 at close of the market at 3.30 PM same day. For this, let's have a look at the option chain prices at the close of market.

CALLS									PUTS							
Volume	IV	LTP	Net Chng	Bid Qty	Bid Price	Ask Price	Ask Qty	Strike Price	Bid Qty	Bid Price	Ask Price	Ask Qty	Net Chng	LTP	IV	Volume
71	25.23	786.90	223.90	75	782.00	790.15	75	8600.00	75	81.35	82.50	2,775	-55.60	82.00	33.03	8,118
-	-	-	-	75	703.90	769.60	75	8650.00	75	83.10	93.10	150	-60.70	90.05	33.01	382
238	21.96	695.15	204.55	75	698.60	706.45	75	8700.00	75	98.60	99.00	75	-66.65	98.40	32.68	9,323
-	-	-	-	75	573.35	708.90	75	8750.00	75	109.00	117.95	75	-89.95	109.05	-	27
816	22.60	614.85	191.05	75	614.85	627.70	75	8800.00	75	117.00	117.85	300	-80.10	117.05	32.52	13,084
-	-	-	-	75	543.45	665.50	75	8850.00	75	121.05	134.90	75	-1,486.00	128.00	-	3
1,284	23.34	548.05	186.35	75	541.50	549.80	75	8900.00	75	140.50	141.20	75	-91.10	141.00	31.93	7,396
-	-	-	-	-	-	524.70	75	8950.00	225	107.95	159.40	225	-94.60	156.00	32.59	70
16,179	22.64	471.05	170.95	75	471.00	474.80	75	9000.00	900	167.95	168.00	1,200	-105.10	168.00	31.71	31,613
377	22.71	435.00	161.30	75	419.00	509.50	75	9050.00	375	165.25	188.95	150	-105.05	186.60	30.86	516
8,676	22.74	402.05	154.20	75	402.70	407.00	75	9100.00	75	200.00	200.95	750	-119.65	200.05	31.77	9,565
195	24.01	363.55	136.10	75	234.10	452.55	7,350	9150.00	150	208.65	222.00	75	-49.45	214.85	-	105
13.009	22.83	344.75	142.40	150	338.00	346.00	75	9200.00	450	238.00	238.95	750	-133.25	238.00	31.57	8,360
103	-	315.00	-1,075.60	75	311.00	325.40	150	9250.00	75	253.00	263.80	225	-1,598.05	258.75	-	111
14,626	22.71	286.45	124.35	75	287.00	288.00	1,575	9300.00	75	280.35	281.95	750	-150.40	282.00	31.33	5,315
48	-	264.40	-1,090.65	75	256.05	350.90	75	9350.00	75	300.00	319.60	150	-1,600.75	319.00	-	1
15,492	22.81	235.00	106.40	75	235.00	238.05	300	9400.00	75	323.45	329.95	750	-172.50	324.35	32.90	906
9	-	215.00	85.00	75	210.20	264.00	225	9450.00	75	333.85	452.60	75	-219.45	350.00	30.97	7
33,582	22.98	191.90	90.90	75	190.85	192.00	3,900	9500.00	75	386.00	388.40	750	-182.45	388.00	33.30	11,541
50	-	159.40	72.40	75	100.05	190.75	225	9550.00	75	303.25	452.55	75	-1,623.15	425.00	-	2
10,031	23.01	152.05	73.10	75	152.00	155.45	75	9600.00	75	442.70	447.95	750	-198.35	442.70	34.15	239
-	-	-	-	150	128.30	-	-	9650.00	75	285.85	571.50	75	-	-	-	-

The Last Trading Price of the put of 9200 was 238.50 and the Last Trading Price of put of 8900 was 141. That means, had you covered your positions in intraday itself just after 2 hours and 20 minutes, you would have incurred loss on put of 9200 (that you had bought at 307.20) for selling the same at 238.50, amounting to 307.20 – 238.50 = 68.70 × 75 = 5152.50 rupees. Also, you had sold 2 puts of 8900 at 185.95 and you would have to buy the same now at 141 to cover your position, thus making a profit of 185.95 – 141.00 = 44.95 × 2 = 89.90 × 75 = 6742.50 rupees. Thus, within 2 hours and 30 minutes, you would have made a profit of 6742.50 on puts sold and incurred loss of 5152.50 on the put bought. In other words, had you closed your positions in intraday itself, you would have earned an amount of 6742.50 – 5152.50 = 1590 rupees in just 2 hours 30 minutes.

This way, if you had pledged your NIFTY ETF units and created the spread like above just for 2 hours, you could have earned Rs. 1590. The possibility of loss was very minimal. That day, NIFTY had gone up and closed at 9314.95; that would have also increased the value of your NIFTY ETF holding besides giving you the opportunity to use the spread to make Rs. 1590 with margin.

3. Call Ratio Backspread: This is the opposite of call ratio spread. We write 1 In the Money call and use the premium received from the same for buying 2 Out of the Money calls such that we are still left with some balance of premium. Let's have a look at the NIFTY option chain at 1 PM on 27 May, 2020 (with expiry of 25 June, 2020) again.

CALLS									PUTS							
Volume	IV	LTP	Net Chng	Bid Qty	Bid Price	Ask Price	Ask Qty	Strike Price	Bid Qty	Bid Price	Ask Price	Ask Qty	Net Chng	LTP	IV	Volume
38	25.23	626.65	63.65	375	640.35	648.85	375	8600.00	75	108.30	108.55	75	-29.05	108.55	33.03	3,147
-	-	-	-	4,950	587.90	613.30	4,950	8650.00	75	115.45	121.35	75	-32.25	118.50	33.01	363
105	21.96	565.00	74.40	75	563.80	568.85	75	8700.00	225	129.80	130.20	75	-35.45	129.60	32.68	4,444
-	-	-	-	4,950	512.10	537.50	4,950	8750.00	75	137.90	145.45	75	-56.15	142.85	-	9
414	22.60	492.35	68.55	75	491.35	494.30	75	8800.00	225	156.10	156.65	75	-40.75	156.40	32.52	6,940
-	-	-	-	4,950	443.95	469.40	4,950	8850.00	4,950	163.20	178.60	75	-	-	-	-
549	23.34	424.55	62.85	150	421.55	423.85	1,125	8900.00	150	185.95	186.15	525	-46.10	186.00	31.93	2,924
-	-	-	-	4,950	374.30	399.25	4,950	8950.00	75	200.20	204.50	75	-44.60	206.00	32.59	32
9,098	22.64	358.00	57.90	75	357.00	357.70	75	9000.00	300	220.50	221.35	75	-52.60	220.50	31.71	13,108
288	22.71	323.90	50.20	75	325.30	327.40	75	9050.00	75	239.05	240.00	75	-49.65	242.00	30.86	168
4,398	22.74	298.00	50.15	75	297.00	297.85	75	9100.00	75	259.90	260.80	75	-59.70	260.00	31.77	3,145
76	24.01	272.50	45.05	75	269.25	273.75	75	9150.00	1,125	281.10	285.05	75	20.75	285.05	-	12
6,070	22.83	244.95	42.60	150	244.35	245.00	75	9200.00	75	305.90	307.20	150	-64.50	306.75	31.57	1,897
-	-	-	-	75	216.20	227.45	600	9250.00	4,950	321.35	345.05	150	-	-	-	-
4,876	22.71	199.10	37.00	75	198.85	199.40	150	9300.00	150	360.00	361.00	75	-72.50	359.90	31.33	271
-	-	-	-	150	165.70	184.90	4,950	9350.00	4,950	376.25	400.95	75	-	-	-	-
4,599	22.81	159.20	30.60	75	158.05	158.75	150	9400.00	300	419.00	421.60	150	-76.85	420.00	32.90	280
1	-	93.20	-36.80	75	101.00	-	-	9450.00	4,950	443.75	464.45	4,950	-36.35	533.10	30.97	1
14,787	22.98	125.25	24.25	75	125.45	125.85	150	9500.00	75	487.55	488.50	75	-81.90	488.55	33.30	2,946

CALLS									PUTS							
Volume	IV	LTP	Net Chng	Bid Qty	Bid Price	Ask Price	Ask Qty	Strike Price	Bid Qty	Bid Price	Ask Price	Ask Qty	Net Chng	LTP	IV	Volume
11	-	104.00	17.00	75	106.30	111.30	75	9550.00	75	511.30	536.20	75	-	-	-	-
4,098	23.01	96.40	17.45	75	96.15	96.50	225	9600.00	450	551.50	558.50	150	-86.05	555.00	34.15	83
-	-	-	-	1,200	28.60	-	-	9650.00	7,350	453.25	685.80	7,350	-	-	-	-
4,422	23.05	72.70	12.85	600	72.60	72.75	75	9700.00	150	624.80	634.70	75	-66.20	648.00	-	6
-	-	-	-	1,200	25.20	88.75	150	9750.00	75	578.45	739.70	75	-	-	-	-
5,097	23.34	53.65	7.45	75	53.45	53.80	225	9800.00	150	706.90	715.15	225	-99.70	716.00	36.68	22
-	-	-	-	1,200	16.20	88.85	150	9850.00	75	711.20	862.75	75	-	-	-	-
2,847	23.60	40.05	4.35	75	39.90	40.10	75	9900.00	150	793.20	801.05	150	-104.85	805.00	31.37	19
-	-	-	-	1,200	14.20	78.35	150	9950.00	525	760.25	923.40	7,425	-	-	-	-
9,782	23.95	29.95	3.05	75	29.85	30.00	4,350	10000.00	150	883.00	888.80	75	-108.30	886.00	39.08	832
-	-	-	-	1,200	9.60	68.40	300	10050.00	7,350	851.20	1,063.65	7,350	-	-	-	-
710	24.00	20.85	0.70	75	20.70	21.20	75	10100.00	225	969.00	980.65	75	-66.25	1,014.95	-	23

You get the premium of Rs. 269.25 for writing In the Money call of 9150. For buying calls of 9550 and 9500 at premiums of 111.30 and 125.85 respectively, you need a total 111.30 + 125.85 = 237.15 rupees, thus leaving you with a premium credit of 269.25 – 237.15 = 32.10 rupees. That means, if NIFTY closes on expiry at any level below 9150, you would surely get 32.10 × 75 = 2407.50 rupees. If you prefer to close positions in intraday only, please have a look at the option chain after 2 hours for expiry of 27 June, 2020.

The Last Trading Price for 9150 is 363.55 and LTP for the call of 9500 is 191.90 and that for the call of 9550 is 159.40. That means, if you close your positions in intraday in 2 hours, you would have profit/loss as below.

1. Loss on short call of 9150 = 363.55 – 269.25 = 94.30 × 75 = 7072.50.
2. Profit on call of 9500 = 191.90 – 125.85 = 66.05 × 75 = 4953.75.
3. Profit on call of 9550 = 159.40 – 111.30 = 48.10 × 75 = 3607.50.
4. Net Profit = 4953.75 + 3607.50 – 7072.50 = 1488.75. That means you are making a profit of 1488.75 in intraday.

Suppose you decided to wait till 18 June, 2020. At noon on 18 June, 2020, LTP of the call of 9150 in NIFTY was 739.30, LTP of the call of 9500 was 505.75 and LTP of the call of 9550 was 418.00. Hence, had you held your positions till 18 June, 2020 and closed them on 18 June, 2020, your profit/loss figures would have been as below.

1. Loss on call writing of 9150 = 739.30 – 269.25 = 470.05 × 75 = 35,253.75.
2. Profit on the call of 9500 = 505.75 – 125.85 = 379.90 × 75 = 28,492.50.

CALLS									PUTS							
Volume	IV	LTP	Net Chng	Bid Qty	Bid Price	Ask Price	Ask Qty	Strike Price	Bid Qty	Bid Price	Ask Price	Ask Qty	Net Chng	LTP	IV	Volume
71	25.23	786.90	223.90	75	782.00	790.15	75	8600.00	75	81.35	82.50	2,775	-55.60	82.00	33.03	8,118
-	-	-	-	75	703.90	769.60	75	8650.00	75	83.10	93.10	150	-60.70	90.05	33.01	382
238	21.96	695.15	204.55	75	698.60	706.45	75	8700.00	75	98.60	99.00	75	-66.65	98.40	32.68	9,323
-	-	-	-	75	573.35	708.90	75	8750.00	75	109.00	117.95	75	-89.95	109.05	-	27
816	22.60	614.85	191.05	75	614.85	627.70	75	8800.00	75	117.00	117.85	300	-80.10	117.05	32.52	13,084
-	-	-	-	75	543.45	665.50	75	8850.00	75	121.05	134.90	75	-1,486.00	128.00	-	3
1,284	23.34	548.05	186.35	75	541.50	549.80	75	8900.00	75	140.50	141.20	75	-91.10	141.00	31.93	7,396
-	-	-	-	-	-	524.70	75	8950.00	225	107.95	159.40	225	-94.60	156.00	32.59	70
16,179	22.64	471.05	170.95	75	471.00	474.80	75	9000.00	900	167.95	168.00	1,200	-105.10	168.00	31.71	31,613
377	22.71	435.00	161.30	75	419.00	509.50	75	9050.00	375	165.25	188.95	150	-105.05	186.60	30.86	516
8,676	22.74	402.05	154.20	75	402.70	407.00	75	9100.00	75	200.00	200.95	750	-119.65	200.05	31.77	9,565
195	24.01	363.55	136.10	75	234.10	452.55	7,350	9150.00	150	208.65	222.00	75	-49.45	214.85	-	105
13,009	22.83	344.75	142.40	150	338.00	346.00	75	9200.00	450	238.00	238.95	750	-133.25	238.00	31.57	8,360
103	-	315.00	-1,075.60	75	311.00	325.40	150	9250.00	75	253.00	263.80	225	-1,598.05	258.75	-	111
14,626	22.71	286.45	124.35	75	287.00	288.00	1,575	9300.00	75	280.35	281.95	750	-150.40	282.00	31.33	5,315
48	-	264.40	-1,090.65	75	256.05	350.90	75	9350.00	75	300.00	319.60	150	-1,600.75	319.00	-	1
15,492	22.81	235.00	106.40	75	235.00	238.05	300	9400.00	75	323.45	329.95	750	-172.50	324.35	32.90	906
9	-	215.00	85.00	75	210.20	264.00	225	9450.00	75	333.85	452.60	75	-219.45	350.00	30.97	7
33,582	22.98	191.90	90.90	75	190.85	192.00	3,900	9500.00	75	386.00	388.40	750	-182.45	388.00	33.30	11,541
50	-	159.40	72.40	75	100.05	190.75	225	9550.00	75	303.25	452.55	75	-1,623.15	425.00	-	2
10,031	23.01	152.05	73.10	75	152.00	155.45	75	9600.00	75	442.70	447.95	750	-198.35	442.70	34.15	239
-	-	-	-	150	128.30	-	-	9650.00	75	285.85	571.50	75	-	-	-	-

3. Profit on the call of 9550 = 418.00 – 111.30 = 306.70 × 75 = 32,002.50.
4. Net profit = 28492.50 + 23002.50 – 35253.75 = 16241.25.

   Thus, you had an opportunity to exit before expiry.

Similarly, under this strategy, different levels of closure on expiry would have resulted in profit/loss figures as below.

Sl. No.	Level of Expiry	P/L on shorted call of 9150	P/L on call of 9500	P/L on call of 9550	Total Profit/Loss
1	Below 9150	2407.50	0	0	2407.50
2	9150	2407.50	0	0	2407.50
3	9200	–1342.50	0	0	–1342.50
4	9250	–5092.50	0	0	–5092.50
5	9300	–8842.50	0	0	–8842.50
6	9350	–12592.50	0	0	–12592.50
7	9400	–16342.50	0	0	–16342.50
8	9450	–20092.50	0	0	–20092.50
9	9500	–23842.50	0	0	–23842.50
10	9550	–27592.50	3750	0	–23842.50
11	9600	–31342.50	7500	3750	–20092.50
12	9650	–35092.50	11250	75000	–16342.50
13	9700	–38842.50	15000	11200	–12592.50
14	9750	–42592.50	18750	15000	–8842.50
15	9800	–46342.50	22500	18750	–5092.50
16	9850	–50092.50	26250	22500	–1342.50

Thus, you may see that this method works reasonably well in intraday and your maximum loss is limited when you hold the positions till expiry. Overall, this method is safer compared to buying or writing naked calls, and if you close positions in intraday itself, it results in profit or limited loss.

4. Put Ratio Backspread: This also is opposite to put ratio spread i.e. 1 In the Money put is written and out of the

CALLS									PUTS							
Volume	IV	LTP	Net Chng	Bid Qty	Bid Price	Ask Price	Ask Qty	Strike Price	Bid Qty	Bid Price	Ask Price	Ask Qty	Net Chng	LTP	IV	Volume
38	25.23	626.65	63.65	375	640.35	648.85	375	8600.00	75	108.30	108.55	75	-29.05	108.55	33.03	3,147
-	-	-	-	4,950	587.90	613.30	4,950	8650.00	75	115.45	121.35	75	-32.25	118.50	33.01	363
105	21.96	565.00	74.40	75	563.80	568.85	75	8700.00	225	129.80	130.20	75	-35.45	129.60	32.68	4,444
-	-	-	-	4,950	512.10	537.50	4,950	8750.00	75	137.90	145.45	75	-56.15	142.85	-	9
414	22.60	492.35	68.55	75	491.35	494.30	75	8800.00	225	156.10	156.65	75	-40.75	156.40	32.52	6,940
-	-	-	-	4,950	443.95	469.40	4,950	8850.00	4,950	163.20	178.60	75	-	-	-	-
549	23.34	424.55	62.85	150	421.55	423.85	1,125	8900.00	150	185.95	186.15	525	-46.10	186.00	31.93	2,924
-	-	-	-	4,950	374.30	399.25	4,950	8950.00	75	200.20	204.50	75	-44.60	206.00	32.59	32
9,098	22.64	358.00	57.90	75	357.00	357.70	75	9000.00	300	220.50	221.35	75	-52.60	220.50	31.71	13,108
288	22.71	323.90	50.20	75	325.30	327.40	75	9050.00	75	239.05	240.00	75	-49.65	242.00	30.86	168
4,398	22.74	298.00	50.15	75	297.00	297.85	75	9100.00	75	259.90	260.80	75	-59.70	260.00	31.77	3,145
76	24.01	272.50	45.05	75	269.25	273.75	75	9150.00	1,125	281.10	285.05	75	20.75	285.05	-	12
6,070	22.83	244.95	42.60	150	244.35	245.00	75	9200.00	75	305.90	307.20	150	-64.50	306.75	31.57	1,897
-	-	-	-	75	216.20	227.45	600	9250.00	4,950	321.35	345.05	150	-	-	-	-
4,876	22.71	199.10	37.00	75	198.85	199.40	150	9300.00	150	360.00	361.00	75	-72.50	359.90	31.33	271
-	-	-	-	150	165.70	184.90	4,950	9350.00	4,950	376.25	400.95	75	-	-	-	-
4,599	22.81	159.20	30.60	75	158.05	158.75	150	9400.00	300	419.00	421.60	150	-76.85	420.00	32.90	280
1	-	93.20	-36.80	75	101.00	-	-	9450.00	4,950	443.75	464.45	4,950	-36.35	533.10	30.97	1
14,787	22.98	125.25	24.25	75	125.45	125.85	150	9500.00	75	487.55	488.50	75	-51.90	488.55	33.30	2,946
11	-	104.00	17.00	75	106.30	111.30	75	9550.00	75	511.30	536.20	75	-	-	-	-
4,098	23.01	96.40	17.45	75	96.15	96.50	225	9600.00	450	551.50	558.50	150	-86.05	555.00	34.15	83
-	-	-	-	1,200	28.60	-	-	9650.00	7,350	453.25	685.80	7,350	-	-	-	-
4,422	23.05	72.70	12.85	600	72.60	72.75	75	9700.00	150	624.80	634.70	75	-66.20	648.00	-	6
-	-	-	-	1,200	25.20	88.75	150	9750.00	75	578.45	739.70	75	-	-	-	-
5,097	23.34	53.65	7.45	75	53.45	53.80	225	9800.00	150	706.90	715.15	225	-99.70	716.00	36.68	22
-	-	-	-	1,200	16.20	88.85	150	9850.00	75	711.20	862.75	75	-	-	-	-
2,847	23.60	40.05	4.35	75	39.90	40.10	75	9900.00	150	793.20	801.05	150	-104.85	805.00	31.37	19
-	-	-	-	1,200	14.20	78.35	150	9950.00	525	760.25	923.40	7,425	-	-	-	-
9,782	23.95	29.95	3.05	75	29.85	30.00	4,350	10000.00	150	883.00	888.80	75	-108.30	886.00	39.08	832
-	-	-	-	1,200	9.60	68.40	300	10050.00	7,350	851.20	1,063.65	7,350	-	-	-	-
710	24.00	20.85	0.70	75	20.70	21.20	75	10100.00	225	969.00	980.65	75	-66.25	1,014.95	-	23

premium received for the same, 2 Out of the Money puts are bought. For example, please look at the option chain at 1 PM on 27 May, 2020.

We would have received premium of 305.90 at bid price for selling put of 9200. Against that, for buying 2 puts of 8700 and 8650, we would have spent 130.20 + 121.35 = 251.55 at their 'ask prices'. Thus, we would have got a credit of 305.90 – 251.55 = 54.35 × 75 = 4076.25 rupees. Had NIFTY remained above 9200 till expiry, this 4076.25 would have been ours. NIFTY was anyway above 10,000 on 18 June, 2020 and hence, this profit was maintained till 18 June, 2020. Now, I am not going to give you calculations for the profit/loss figures for different levels of NIFTY in Intraday and on expiry. I feel by now you know the process and you may yourself calculate all those profit / loss figures.

Summary: In short, I mean to say that once you have accumulated NIFTY ETF units for over Rs. 7 lacs through regular SIP i.e. by planting a money tree, you should first of all write a covered call of value 5% above current price to lock 5% growth and the premium received for the same.

After that, if it's possible, pledge your ETF units to avail margin and use the same to create all the four spreads viz. Call Ratio Spread, Put Ratio Spread, Call Ratio Backspread and Put Ratio Backspread on daily basis. Close all your positions in intraday and take whatever profit or loss they result into. When you create all the four spreads, you should definitely earn some profit irrespective of the direction the market moves. If you are not able to get enough margin to create all the four spreads, you may go for one or two or three spreads as per your need. In my view, Covered Call and Ratio Spread are the safest methods for making money with options; rest of the trading methods are in any case always risky.

□

Conclusion

Thanks for reading my book till the end. Possibly, you may be feeling that I have not told you about many of the strategies in options. Some readers may say that I have not discussed anything about 'Iron Condor' strategy, 'Synthetic Long' and 'Arbitrage', 'Bear Call Ladder', 'Bear Put Spread', 'Bear Call Spread', 'Long Straddle', 'Short Straddle' etc.

Before answering that, I would like to ask you a question, "Have you ever played cards?" If your answer is yes, you know that if you show your cards to the opponent and declare that you are going to win, the probability of your win is limited to 5% to 10% only. If you play the game with your cards exposed to the opponent, he would try to play in a way so as to ensure your defeat.

The same thing applies to option trading. As the date of expiry is fixed in this case, there is only one theory that is predominant here irrespective of the kind of strategy you use. And that is 'Pain Theory' or 'Max Pain Theory'. In other words, large traders can watch your positions and they have the capacity to buy or sell stocks in large quantities so as to manipulate option settlement in such a way that the same generates maximum pain for you i.e. maximum of your money is transferred to their accounts.

If you are fresh in the market, it is possible that you sometimes make some profits using many of these strategies but, as you progress and increase your positions, the impact of this pain theory would start getting felt. You would then start losing money in these strategies and then start exploring some other safer methods. That is why, there are so many strategies suggested for options that, even if you were a great mathematician, the pain theory alone would be enough to fail your knowledge of mathematics.

Hence, it is not the purpose of my book to confuse you with a number of theoretical strategies. The gist of the knowledge that I have imparted is that, if you want to earn regular and safe income from options, you should necessarily take up the following 8 activities.

A money tree in NIFTY/Bank NIFTY ETF as explained in previous chapters will have to be planted.

An SIP of at least Rs. 5000 per week will have to be started and continued as fertiliser for that tree.

This tree will have to be trimmed and pruned regularly while enjoying its tax-free fruits.

Now, you have to keep writing covered calls of 5% above current prices in NIFTY/NIFTY BeES and keep earning safe weekly premiums as rent for the shade of that tree. Keep increasing the number of covered calls as the tree grows; this will gradually increase your income.

If market goes up by 5%, you would get ample quantity of fruits and you would be in profit only.

Even if the market goes down, the amount that you earn from premium on covered calls would be more than bank interest. In fact, the income may sometimes surprise you. Many a time, the market may go up and then fall and then you would enjoy both tax-free fruits as well as premium as rent for sitting in the shade of that tree.

Besides above, you have to just work with the methods of call put ratio spread that I have discussed in previous chapters, as they will give you pain only when there is a large jump or deep decline; you would be able to make money almost safely otherwise.

If you want to use 4-stroke method in NIFTY/Bank NIFTY, you should do that only in intraday or for 5 minutes only; you should not hold overnight a position in option created using 4-stroke method. Let me explain this. There is a kid named Bhavyu in my neighbourhood. He is right now learning counting. If you ask him to count, he would count one, two, three, four and jump to seven, eight, nine and then count as twelve, fifteen, four, three etc. If you tell him that his counting is wrong, he would insist that his counting is right.

In my opinion also, his counting is right and we only don't know counting, as when NIFTY closes at 9720 at night, it may open next day with a gap-up straight at 10,140. As per normal counting, it should have started with trades either at 9720 or 9721.

Similarly, besides gap-up opening (like 4 to 7 straightaway), there may be gap-down (from 15 to four) opening also. That means, from a last night's position of 10630, it may open next day even at 9940. Hence, if you create positions using 4-stroke method and you don't close them either through stop loss or otherwise within 5 minutes or maximum in the intraday, a gap-up or gap-down opening may result in your entire premium getting wiped out overnight.

Above 8 methods only have been found by me to be the safest. If you still want to read some more details, you may do a search on Google for Zerodha Varsity website. Zerodha has made available notes on options in Hindi and English in very simple language. You may read them for free. They are so nicely presented with explanations that you may not even feel the need to read any other book on options.

There is a Zerodha Varsity app also, though this app does not have notes on options in Hindi. However, as per Zerodha, notes in Hindi are soon going to be provided in this app. Lastly, I would like to offer my apology if I have made any error or omission while writing this book. No knowledge is ever complete. Now, it is your turn to use your intelligence and prudence and test these methods against your own criteria. It is now time for you to evaluate this book that is the outcome of my three years' hard work, and give your *'Gurudakshina'* for the same. I am just asking for your review as your *'Gurudakshina'* (I am not going to make an improper demand for a positive review; I am just requesting you to evaluate honestly and I would welcome both positive and negative reviews).

May that Supreme Power whom you know as Bhagawan, God, Allah, Wahe Guru or any other name bless us all and may good sense prevail upon all.

Yours,

—Mahesh Chandra Kaushik

□□□